SOUTH DAKOTA
MINNESOT
DeSmet
Walnut Gro
MISSOURI
RIVER
IOWA
MISSISSIPPI
RIVER
N
W
E
S
NEBRASKA
MISSOURI
KANSAS
Independence
Mansfield
OKLAHOMA

"I Remember Laura"

"I Remember Laura"

Laura Ingalls Wilder

STEPHEN W. HINES

THOMAS NELSON PUBLISHERS

Nashville · Atlanta · London · Vancouver

For Megan, Laura, and Amy—so dear to my heart

Published in Nashville, Tennessee, by Thomas Nelson, Inc., Publishers, and distributed in Canada by Word Communications, Ltd., Richmond, British Columbia, and in the United Kingdom by Word (UK), Ltd., Milton Keynes, England.

Library of Congress Cataloging-in-Publication Data

Hines, Stephen W.
I remember Laura / by Stephen W. Hines.
p. cm.
ISBN 0-7852-8206-8
1. Wilder, Laura Ingalls, 1867–1957—Homes and haunts—South Dakota—De Smet.
2. Women authors, American—20th century—Biography. 3. De Smet (S.D.)—Social life and customs. I. Title.
PS3545.I342Z67 1994
813'.52—dc20
[B] 94-12898
CIP

Printed in the United States of America

1 2 3 4 5 6—99 98 97 96 95 94

Contents

PART 4: REFLECTIONS

APPENDICES

Acknowledgments

A book of this sort is made up of the work of many helping hands. I can only acknowledge a few of the dozens upon dozens of people who have contributed toward making this book happen.

For their interviews or for general help in pointing me toward places where I could find information about Laura Ingalls Wilder, I wish to thank James A. Lichty, Iola Jones, Roscoe Jones, and Sheldon Jones, Neta Seal, Nava Austin, Larry Dennis, Erman and Peggy Dennis, Sondra Gray, Madge Matlock, Suzanne Lippard, Mrs. M. J. Huffman, Mrs. Tom Carter, Don Brazeal, Imogene Green, Darrell Hunter, the Reverend and Mrs. Carleton Knight, Alvie Turner, Tom Carnall, Mrs. Floyd Cooley, Debbie Von Behren, W. D. Le Count, Arlen Le Count, Paul and Arlene Magnin, Alvin Goldberg, Francis G. Thayer, Donald Harding, Aleene Kindel, Dorothy A. Buenemann, Mrs. Florence Vanderneut, Lois Morris, Betty Haskell, Emogene Fuge, Addie Paradise, Professor Elliott Hollister, and Professor Ann Thomas Moore. I hope I will be forgiven if I have left anyone out.

I wish also to thank L Z Drummond, my brother-in-law, for his research work. These people were also vital to my research: Dwight M. Miller, Senior Archivist, Herbert Hoover Presidential Library; Jim E. Detlefsen, audio-visual department, Herbert Hoover Presidential Library; Connie Dowcett, copyright administrator, the *Christian Science Monitor*: Clyde A. Rowan, President of the Wright County Historical and Genealogical Society; Dr. Leon Raney, Dean of Libraries, South Dakota State University; Laura Glum, Archivist, South Dakota State Archives; LaVera Rose, Manuscript Curator, South Dakota State Historical Society; Fae Sotham, Editorial Secretary, The

State Historical Society of Missouri; Nancy Sherbert, Curator of Photographs, Kansas State Historical Society; and Darrell Garwood, audio-visual collection, Kansas State Historical Society.

I wish to thank photographers Brett Coomber of the *Independence Daily Reporter*, Independence, Kansas; Franklin Robertson; and Arlene Magnin. Thanks to The Bettmann Archive for photos related to World War I, and thanks to Andy McMills for permission to use a photograph from the *Springfield-News-Leader*.

For their editorial skills I wish to thank Janet Thoma, Susan Salmon Trotman, Laurie Clark, and Brian Hampton of Janet Thoma Books.

Also my thanks to Michael S. Hyatt, my agent.

Part 1

Laura

CHAPTER 1

Kindred Souls: A Reason for Reminiscence

It was one of those rare days when we weren't particularly rushed by our competing job schedules, a lull in the constant storm of two recent newlyweds who spent a lot of time saying, "Hello. Good-bye. I must be going!"

I was trying to get a start in journalism and creative writing, and my wife was making this large endeavor possible by working as a librarian at a middle school (whatever that is; we had junior high schools when I was young).

The one thing that made our busy schedules bearable—because we would have preferred being together to being apart—was that we read to each other. I have no idea how many books we experienced this way, but because my wife worked with books and I dreamed of writing them, reading to each other kept us together in a special world of the imagination. We both agreed with Emily Dickinson who said, "There is no frigate like a book to take us lands away." Not that we were so much escaping anything as we were resting from the "tyranny of the urgent."

One day while we were discussing our favorite books, I mentioned to my wife, Gwen, that one of the special privileges I had had as a boy attending one- and two-room school houses was that I had been able to read the books by Laura Ingalls Wilder—about eight to ten times in fact.

"You what?" she exclaimed in amazement. "Why you hardly ever read a book a second time. Not since I've known you. Aren't those girls' books?"

"Not at all," I said a little defensively. "Why, they are wonderful books for anybody, and I found them on the shelf of our four-shelf library at school. Have you read any of them?"

"Well, not exactly," my wife admitted. "I just know they are constantly checked out and that our library copies are getting threadbare. Of course, I've read articles about them in library journals, and I've seen the TV

series, but that makes me cry until I get a headache. By the way, do you think Melissa Gilbert looks anything like the real Laura?"

Suddenly, I was seized with a mission. Here was one of America's great (though unknown) librarians, and she hadn't read a Laura Ingalls Wilder book! In her imagination, Pa Ingalls looked like Michael Landon. To me, it seemed a sacrilege that my well-educated wife might confuse "Little Joe Cartwright" with the real Charles Ingalls.

South Dakota State Historical Society

"Ma"—Caroline Lake Quinter Ingalls

The next day I had the old yellow boxed set of the books sitting on our shelf, and I was reading out loud the opening words to chapter one of *Little House in the Big Woods.*[1]

As I read, we revisited an era when the only competition for family members' time together was the daily round of work, which in its own way fostered the development of the home. And as we were swept along, Gwen and I relived the emotions we associated with our own home backgrounds—love, laughter, tears, and the fellowship of kindred hearts.

Of course, my wife loved the books. Few readers have not become enthralled when they entered Laura's domain. Gwen's heart ached with sadness as the Ingallses decided to leave the security of their home in the woods for the great unknown of the Kansas prairie. She stared in surprise as her usually stoic husband burst into tears reading of Mr. Edwards' bringing

[1]"Little House" is a trademark of HarperCollins Publishers Inc.

Christmas to the Ingalls children in *Little House on the Prairie.* A bright shiny penny, a tin cup, a stick of candy, and the fact that Mr. Edwards had to ford a dangerous river to bring Christmas to the Ingalls girls has come to symbolize much of what Christmas giving really is for my wife and me.

And neither one of us has ever quite gotten over Mary's going blind. It seemed so unfair. How could a family who had already endured so much have this happen to them? The story is told so straightforwardly and bravely, we felt as if that tragedy had befallen someone in our own family. When we finally came to the end of *These Happy Golden Years,* we felt as though we must be kindred souls with that beloved pioneer family.

South Dakota State Historical Society

"Pa"—Charles Philip Ingalls

We had not endured a history lesson; instead, we had become true friends of theirs, baptized into the sacrament of what someone has called "immortal longings." Love should last through every test. Good should win over evil. At the end of life there is the comfort of life everlasting. Pa, Ma, Mary, Laura, Carrie, and Grace could never die.

In the next years, however, the tyranny of the urgent again caught us. Sentiment is no bulwark against the demands of ever present work and worry and the addition to our family of three daughters, including twins. I pursued a publishing career until I was worn out by something that had started out to be a joy and had ended up in the misery of increasing financial obligations.

The founding family of the town of De Smet, South Dakota. Ma and Pa Ingalls and the girls—from left to right—Caroline Lake Quinter Ingalls, Caroline (Carrie) Celestia Ingalls, Laura Elizabeth Ingalls, Charles Philip Ingalls, Grace Pearl Ingalls, and Mary Amelia Ingalls.

That's when Laura entered my life again. One day I came rushing home with the news that Mrs. Wilder had published much more than either my wife or I had ever known. Gwen listened patiently as I explained to her that Mrs. Wilder had written a column, "The Farm Home," in the *Missouri Ruralist*, a paper with a circulation of 100,000 whose purpose was to foster agriculture throughout that state. No doubt there were many undiscovered nuggets of great wisdom by this lady as she had written this column for farmers' wives. Wouldn't several million Wilder fans enjoy such a discovery?

Gwen tried to keep me from hyperventilating. "What makes you think the columns are any good? You haven't even seen them, and you don't

know what they are about. Chances are, there is nothing in them of interest to today's woman, or at least not enough to make a book."

I felt the sense of her disturbingly sound reasoning. What would a middle-aged lady of the early nineteen hundreds have to say to us? Life then couldn't have much connection to life now.

That was only a couple of years ago. Since the publication of these columns in the book *Little House in the Ozarks,* our doubts seem silly. What did she have to say, indeed? The book shot to the best-seller charts and has sold over 300,000 copies. What is better, Laura Ingalls Wilder's fans were not silent in voicing what they had found. These fans wrote:

We all feel part of Laura's special family.

- *"I believe there is wisdom here in these writings that needs to be taken to heart today. . . . I keep returning to her year after year."*
- *"Laura's wit and wisdom are timeless and make sense today, as always. She had a unique, easy way of writing. It all seemed obvious, yet few said the things she said."*
- *"I have made myself read this book slowly. It is so surprising how all the things that Laura Ingalls Wilder said years ago are true today. Thanks for bringing this adult-woman side of Mrs. Wilder to us."*

Laura has always held a special place in the hearts of her millions of readers who feel as though they know her personally, either through her classic books, which were first published during the 1930s, or through the television series of the '70s and early '80s, which may have caused them to first pick up *Little House in the Big Woods* or *Farmer Boy* and begin their reader's journey.

I am a kindred soul with these letter writers, I thought. Though we don't know each other and though we come from vastly different backgrounds, we all feel part of Laura's special family. Ma and Pa and Mary and Laura and Carrie and Grace—and even Jack, the brindle bulldog—never seem to leave us once they have entered our lives. Their companionship is forever in our memory, and we can never believe they are really gone or from a place called Long Ago.

I felt a growing dilemma. My correspondents, whether recent converts or long-time followers of Mrs. Wilder, expressed a common sentiment: "We would like to know still more of this lady and her family—if more information could be found."

Mrs. Florence Vanderneut of Earlville, New York, wrote: "I, too, felt as you that I had found a 'friend' in Laura Ingalls Wilder. I also was 'sad' that after the Little House series there would be no more of her writings. . . . [But] thanks for bringing her back through these collected columns."

Lois Morris of Brookfield, New York, wrote: "All of us who love Laura's writing[s] are eager for more. I always hated to see the end of any of her books."

I shrugged, feeling that I could do nothing to answer their wishes.

Then a question came to mind. Had anyone at the University of Missouri, or at some other school, conducted interviews with the people who knew Mrs. Wilder from her Mansfield, Missouri, days, the days of her final home?

Mrs. Wilder had died in 1957, and surely, I thought, someone would have done this work at the optimum time, right after her death. When phone inquiries turned up no such project, I realized that there was no oral biography of Laura Ingalls Wilder.

A great opportunity had been lost, but I began to believe that I might be able to rectify such an oversight. Although time was running out with each passing year, I could still gather what remained of the collective memory of Laura in and around the small towns where she spent her adult life from the age of twenty-seven to her ninetieth year. My sense of urgency

and purpose was only heightened by knowing that fact and fiction about Laura's life had already become blurred, and I agreed with those who wanted her real story, which was fantastic enough, to shine through.

My quest seemed so simple, now that I look back on it. I talked to as many people as possible, but as I went along, I found a written piece here, another bit of a document there, until I realized that what I had was really a mosaic of the many elements that make up Laura's story: memories not just of herself but of her husband, the silent Almanzo, and her daughter, the gifted and difficult Rose. I couldn't leave those out!

"Homekeeping hearts are happiest."

Neva Whaley Harding had written a small memoir of the settling of De Smet (where Laura's family were first citizens), of living through the "Hard Winter," of knowing the Ingalls family, and of knowing Rob and Ella Boast, prominent characters in *By the Shores of Silver Lake* and *Little Town on the Prairie.*

No, I couldn't leave Mrs. Harding out just because I hadn't talked to her, so I expanded my project to include all sorts of things—anything that could possibly shed light on Mrs. Wilder and her times. Thus, this volume, *"I Remember Laura,"* has become a cornucopia, a Thanksgiving feast—complete with recipes!—of Mrs. Wilder's incredible life and times.

Here you will find newspaper stories, both by and about Mrs. Wilder, as well as the personal interviews that stimulated me to gather old-time recipes, seek out old writings, and hunt further for every scrap of remembrance that might throw light on her. Friends and neighbors, close and not so close, illuminate this lady whose life typified this motto: "Homekeeping hearts are happiest."

I have organized this potpourri of reminiscences chronologically: first, there is a glimpse of Laura's life on the Kansas plains; then come references to Laura's years in De Smet; then her early life in Mansfield is examined; and, finally, her later years are recalled as new questions have been raised about Mrs. Wilder and her daughter.

You might want to glance through this book to see what interests you most. Perhaps the most fascinating part of her early life was the time she spent growing up in De Smet. Her reminiscence of those days, penned for a national newspaper, shows how memory may stand still while time doesn't.

The pictures of Laura's home and the article about how the house "grew like Topsy" as Almanzo built additions are in chapter four. Laura's thought provoking articles about World War I are in chapter nine.

The relationship between her daughter, Rose, and herself, which has recently been the center of so much controversy—"Did Rose edit or rewrite her mother's books? Was their relationship as strained as some insist—is discussed in chapter eleven.

Finally, if you are an avid fan of her children's books, you might enjoy appendix one—the factual accounts in the De Smet paper of familiar characters such as the Reverend E. H. Alden, Laura's favorite minister; of the Boasts, Rob and Ella, who were close friends of the Ingallses; or you might enjoy appendix two, which contains Laura's Mansfield obituary and a reflection by a Mansfield writer.

Let's begin with a brief survey of the Ingallses' early life in De Smet. Here, then, is my varicolored bouquet that once more brings Laura to us. SH

Reminiscences of Laura's Life in De Smet, South Dakota

CHAPTER 2

Long Ago and Far Away: The De Smet Era

Although there are tens of thousands of small western towns dotting this country—all of them with a pioneer past and cast of characters—only one town really stands out with any distinctiveness in American literature: De Smet, South Dakota. For Laura Ingalls Wilder readers, officially numbered in the tens of millions by now, this pioneer prairie town has sprung to life, out of almost nothing, as the "Little Town on the Prairie." De Smet and its environs are the setting for five of Mrs. Wilder's classic books.

Yet such is the power of television that if you surveyed the vast body of American TV viewers they might well name that town as Walnut Grove, Minnesota. That's where Michael Landon and the rest of the cast of the television series entertained viewers for over ten years. For those viewers, Walnut Grove was the archetypal prairie town our forefathers settled. That's TV for you. (Michael Landon did great things for the sale of Laura's books, but he had to conform his vision to modern viewers' desire for photogenic characters.)

A remembrance of Mrs. Wilder must begin in De Smet, South Dakota, the place that forged Laura's personality. A brief list of the events that occurred in De Smet shows you their importance both to Laura and to her stories:

Early in 1879	Pa Ingalls moves to Dakota Territory to work for the Chicago & Northwestern railroad.
September 1879	The Ingalls family settles near Silver Lake.
Later in 1879	The Ingallses move into a surveyors' house for the winter.
Spring 1880	The family moves to their homestead claim south of De Smet.

October 1880	The Ingallses move in to Pa's store in town after the first blizzard of what is to be the Long Winter.
November 1881	Mary leaves for the Iowa School for the Blind in Vinton, Iowa.
December 1882	Laura receives her teacher's certificate and teaches at Brewster school. Although a short term, it is a miserable experience.
1884	Almanzo Wilder proposes to Laura, who is seventeen.
August 25, 1885	Laura and Almanzo marry at the Reverend Edward Brown's home, without any members of Laura's family being present.
December 5, 1886	The couple's daughter, Rose, is born.
Summer 1888	Laura and Almanzo's baby boy, who is never named, dies after living two weeks. They have no more children.
August 1889	Laura and Almanzo's house burns. Laura blames herself.

In May of 1890 Laura and Almanzo moved to Spring Valley, Minnesota, with Almanzo's folks. They lived there—except for a brief sojourn in Florida—for four years until September of 1894 when they moved to Mansfield, Missouri, the town in which they spent the rest of their lives.

Laura lived in De Smet, South Dakota, for eleven years, a long time for the wandering Ingalls family. I begin the De Smet recollections with a poem Laura wrote in 1930, when she was unable to attend the Old Settlers' Day celebration that marked the fiftieth anniversary of the founding of the town. Next is an article titled "The Land of Used to Be," written for the *Christian Science Monitor* in 1940 when she was able to attend the Old Settlers' Day celebration.

Finally we hear the personal recollections of Neva Harding, another

Photo by Franklin Robertson

The home Pa Ingalls built for his family in De Smet

child of the prairie and a close friend of Laura's sister, Carrie. She gives us another view of the town and the Hard Winter of 1880. It was a badge of distinction to have lived through that long winter; it was a badge of distinction to have been among the town's first settlers; it was a badge of distinction to have participated in the struggle to wrest a living from the dry Dakota plains.

Chapter three contains the prize recipes of the founders of the "Little Town on the Prairie," including that of Mrs. C. P. Ingalls, Laura's mother. We have adapted these recipes to today's measurements.

Let's begin by letting Laura tell us, in her own words, what the Dakota prairies meant to her. SH

Dakota Prairies

A POEM BY LAURA INGALLS WILDER

Nobody knows when Laura first began writing poetry, but it was her habit from an early age to put down her feelings in verse. An unpublished collection of Laura's poetry shows that the youthful poet had a good sense of humor, strong opinions, and a sensitive eye for landscape. Although the beauties of nature are frequently extolled in her verse, she was quite versatile, and in later years composed a song for her beloved Athenian Club.

The fact is, poetry for common people was much more in vogue during Laura's early years than it is today. Practically every newspaper from great to small published verse, and there were numerous women's magazines to which one might contribute.

Laura was already well established as a journalist when she penned the following for the De Smet town celebration of Old Settlers' Day.

The poem is preceded by a couple of paragraphs taken from a De Smet News *article about the various settlers who were unable to come for the 1930 celebration that marked fifty years since the settling of the town and the hard winter of 1880-81. The poem itself appeared a week later in the June 20, 1930, edition of the newspaper.*

The paper explains: "Mrs. Wilder, formerly Laura Ingalls, and mother of Rose Wilder Lane, the writer, sent a contribution to the half-century literature [a compilation of authentic pioneer accounts of the prairie's settlement fifty years earlier], a poem giving her first impressions of the vicinity of De Smet in 1879, when her parents came to the banks of Silver Lake to make their home in a railroad camp." SH

Dakota Prairies

Ever I see them in my mental vision
As first my eyes beheld them years agone;
Clad all in brown with russet shades and golden
Stretching away into the far unknown;
Never a break to mar their sweep of grandeur;
From North to South, from East to West the same,
Save that the East was full of purple shadows,
The West with setting sun was all aflame;
Never a sign of human habitation
To show that man's domain was begun;
The only marks the footpaths of the bison
Made by the herds before their day was done.
The sky downturned a brazen bowl to me,
And clanging with the calls of wild gray geese
Winging their way unto the distant Southland
To 'scape the coming storms and rest in peace.
Ever the winds went whispering o'er the prairies,
Ever the grasses whispered back again,
And then the sun dipped down below the skyline,
And stars lit just the outline of the plain.

The Land of Used to Be

AN ARTICLE IN THE CHRISTIAN SCIENCE MONITOR
BY LAURA INGALLS WILDER
April 4, 1940

By 1940, Mrs. Wilder was seventy-three years old, a "discovered" writer, and quite famous. It would have been understandable if she had diverted her energies toward writing for women and children's publications, which would have been exceedingly eager for her work and generous with their pay.

But by now Laura had caught her vision of completing an eight-volume saga of pioneer life, something that would be unique in our literature. By 1940, she still had three books to go and must have felt the press of time—so much to do, so little time to do it.

Perhaps it was more for Almanzo's sake than for her own—since he was nearly ten years her senior—that they piled into their Chrysler for the last trip they ever made to their South Dakota homeland. Only Laura's sisters Grace and Carrie would be there to greet them. All about them the little town of their memory had changed. Laura commented: "Everywhere we went we recognized faces, but we were surprised to find them old and gray like ourselves, instead of being young as in our memories."

"The Land of Used to Be" expands on Laura's quaint amazement. SH

It was the first of June. The days were lovely, warm, goin-somewhere-days and one morning when the blue haze hung over the Ozark hills, Almanzo said, "Let's go back to De Smet for the Old Settlers' Day celebration. I would like to see the old place and the folks we used to know."

Photo by Franklin Robertson

The surveyors' house just as it was when the Ingallses lived there in 1879

"Let's do," I agreed eagerly, for I had just finished writing *By the Shores of Silver Lake*. "We could see the homestead Pa took so long ago and Carrie and Grace."

Friends thought we should not take such a trip by ourselves. We ought any way to have a driver. They were very tactful but their idea was that we should not go so far from home alone.

We don't think that seventy-three or eighty-two is old and we object to being taken care of.

Almanzo said, "I have driven horses all over that country and the roads to it and I can drive a car there."

"I rode behind those horses with you and I can still ride wherever you can drive," I said.

So we told the man who lives on our farm that we were leaving and didn't know when we would be back. He was very kind and promised to take care of everything while we were away.

We don't think that seventy-three or eighty-two is old and we object to being taken care of.

Off for South Dakota

Then, one early morning, we packed our bags, put them in the trunk of the Chrysler, said goodbye to our pet bulldog and started to South Dakota and the "Land of Used to Be."

It was still early in the morning when we came to Springfield, fifty miles away.

Going into Springfield we took the wrong turn and were some time finding the street that led to the highway we must take. A little way and the street detoured. We took the detour and went on and on.

"Haven't we gone far enough to come to the highway?" Almanzo asked at last.

"It seems like it," I said. "But going east we are bound to find the highway running north." Instead we found ourselves on a country road.

A friendly stranger directed us and soon we saw the highway signs and were on our way.

"This is a good start," I grouched. "Lost twice this early in the morning and our first day out. Do you suppose we will get lost coming and going in every city on our way?"

"It wasn't we were lost. It was the highway," Almanzo said earnestly.

We stopped for lunch at a little eating place beside the road, then went on again in the pleasant afternoon.

When we came to a junction of our highway with one crossing it, we took the wrong end of the new highway. After going a few miles we discovered our mistake, retraced our way, and followed the highway on in the right direction.

"That is three times lost in one day," Almanzo said.

"I think it is the limit," I added.

"We will make it the limit," Almanzo declared. "Three times is enough to be lost in one day."

ON THE PRAIRIE

We drove happily on across the level land of North Missouri and Southwestern Iowa. Then out on the Dakota prairie where meadow larks sang beside the road. The sun shone into the car and the soft spring wind blew in my face. Almost I seemed to hear Ma say, "Laura put your sunbonnet on! You'll look like an Indian." So I tilted my wide hat brim to shield my face from sun and wind.

Late one afternoon we came to De Smet.

The little town we used to know was gone. In its place was a town that spread north beyond the railroad tracks, east to the lake shore, south where the big slough used to be and far to the west. The old schoolhouse was gone. Its place was taken by a large brick school building.

Along Main Street were fine business houses in place of the one story with a two story false front stores of the old days.

A large brick bank with offices above stood on the corner where Pa had built his small office building. We took rooms in a hotel a little way from it.

Next morning at breakfast, two men looked sharply at us as they passed our table, then came back and stopped.

"Hello, Laura," one of them said.

I looked up in surprise into the laughing black eyes of a tall man.

"I am Laura, but who are you?" I answered him.

"I am Sam," he said. "I would know you anywhere." And then I remembered him for an old schoolmate, one of the younger boys in our crowd.

TALK OF OLD TIMES

The other man had known Almanzo well. They joined us at the table and we recalled old times together.

Main Street was full of street fair and it rained. It rained all day but nobody cared. After so many dry years people were happy to be rained on. When a hard shower came they ducked under awnings and into doorways. Between showers they splashed smilingly up and down and across where water was running.

Almanzo and I were crossing the street when I heard someone calling, "Oh, Laura, Laura!" I looked back. Running after us was a little woman.

"I knew you!" she exclaimed. "I knew you!"

"You are Maggie," I said. We stood in the middle of the street—we who had last seen each other as girls in school—and the rain poured down.

Wherever I went someone called, "Laura." It made me feel quite young again. Then I met an old schoolmate with her grandchildren.

We drove out to see Pa's old homestead. There is a nice farmhouse in place of the little claim shanty, but the cottonwood trees we set that long ago day when Grace was lost among the violets are still growing—big trees now.

We drove to a near-by town to see Grace and her husband [Manchester, South Dakota]. From there we drove across the plains to the Black Hills.

Sister Carrie lives in the Black Hills at the foot of Mt. Rushmore, where the great stone faces are carved in the living granite of the mountain top. As we drove the winding roads, those stone likenesses of Washington, Jefferson, Lincoln, and Theodore Roosevelt looked down on us.

Carrie and Grace who used to be my little sisters are now taller than I am. We talked together of childhood days and Pa and Ma and Mary.

When we talked of our return journey, we decided not to go back the way we came. Instead, we drove on to further adventures. But that is another story, for as we drove away from sister Carrie's home, our visit to the Land of Used to Be was ended.

Child of the Prairie

THE PERSONAL RECOLLECTIONS OF NEVA WHALEY HARDING

"Child of the Prairie" Neva Harding (née Whaley) was one of the early pioneers of South Dakota. She and her family arrived in the town of De Smet, South Dakota, in the summer that preceded the famous "Hard Winter" of 1880–81.

That was a summer full of hope. The new community was filling fast with settlers who had already been driven from hearth and home by failures elsewhere. Some had left in the middle of the night to avoid creditors. Some had seen little children die on the way. These folks hoped that the Dakota Territory would be their stopping place, the bustling beginnings of De Smet a good omen of their own fresh start as well.

The Ingalls family—Charles and Caroline and their daughters, Mary, Laura, Carrie, and Grace—important members of the De Smet community, were already settled in a claim shanty just southeast of town. Mutual friends of the Whaley and Ingalls families were the Boasts, Rob and Ella, who had spent the previous winter in a shanty very near the Ingallses'. These stalwart people seemed to offer promise that what was sprouting from the plain was not a mirage but a sturdy community.

Carrie Ingalls became one of Neva Whaley's best friends when they met at the first De Smet school. Their teacher, V. S. L. Owen, had come to teach after the rather unsuccessful tenure of "lazy, lousy 'Liza Jane" Wilder, Almanzo's older, "bossy" sister. Miss Wilder, a pioneer homesteader in her own right, was Laura Ingalls's nemesis for the duration of their teacher/pupil relationship. Later, Laura came to trust Eliza Jane so much that she sent her

daughter, Rose, to live with Eliza so Rose could continue her education at a quality high school in Louisiana.

The following memoir by Neva Whaley Harding, "I Recall Pioneer Days in South Dakota," is a collage of memories of early De Smet. Prominently featuring the Ingallses and the Boasts, it also presents us with another, perhaps grimmer, perspective on the physical and emotional hardships of pioneering than we might expect if we have only read Laura's books, for, inevitably, many fresh hopes were blasted by the reality of the dry Dakota plains. Mrs. Harding's portrait of the loneliness and emotional deterioration of her mother is a sobering tale of what could happen when hope dwindled to a flickering flame. SH

Sometimes very small things decide the path of one's life.

I RECALL PIONEER DAYS IN SOUTH DAKOTA

My father, Josiah Whaley, came to Dakota in the spring of 1880 leaving mother, my four-year-old brother, and me, eight years old, to stay near an uncle in Mantorville, Minnesota. Dad stopped off at various towns along the Chicago & Northwestern Railroad but went on to Huron, the end of the line. Huron gave promise of being a good business town, and Dad felt it would be a good place to locate. But sometimes very small things decide the path of one's life. The water at Huron made him quite ill so he decided to settle at De Smet where, he recalled, the water was fine.

Even at that early date, claims around De Smet had all been filed on, but for a small sum Dad was able to buy a relinquishment on a quarter section three miles east of town.

As the Vermillion River flowed southward, it overflowed into Silver Lake at flood time. On the south bank of the lake, a little south and east of De Smet, lived the Ingalls family. The Boasts told us a lot about the Ingalls

family, having lived with them the winter of 1879–80. I did not meet Laura until later when I attended the De Smet school. (Had I known how famous she was to become, I might have struggled through the tall slough grass among muskrat houses and cattails to her door; might even, perchance, have met her the time she tells of getting lost in that same slough.)

Dad, who liked to work with wood, had owned a sawmill back in Pennsylvania; but, there being no wood to saw in Dakota, he took to building houses. Besides working in De Smet that first summer, he managed to enclose a house for us on the claim and planned to finish it on the inside during the winter. It was rather a good house for those days—two fair-sized rooms and two small ones, several degrees better than a claim shanty. Nearly all houses could be built from lumber shipped in; there was only one sod house in our neighborhood.

Ours was the first train into town after the "Great October Blizzard" of 1880.

THE HARD WINTER

Our house was ready by fall and we took the long, tedious journey from Mantorville, Minnesota, to De Smet by train over a rough roadbed. There were many long waits while snowdrifts were cleared from the track ahead. I, tow-headed Neva, spent most of the time at the backdoor window looking at the monotonous, snow-covered landscape and watching, fascinated, the telegraph poles and iron rails reaching an ever-changing vanishing point in the distance—my first lesson in perspective never to be forgotten. Ours was the first train into town after the "Great October Blizzard" of 1880.

It was dark and after supper when we landed at De Smet. The train was so far off schedule that Dad failed to meet us. Someone kindly piloted us to Charley Mead's hotel, the only one in town, where we found Dad eating a late supper with the hotel help: bright, ambitious girls holding down claims

but working in town for the winter. A Mrs. Remington acted as hostess; she and her husband and little girl, Laura, had also come in from their claim for the winter. Dad was very glad to see us, but he never liked demonstrations of affection; so when I threw my arms around his neck and kissed him and the friendly crowd teased him, he was actually embarrassed.

Dad had been sharing a little shanty a few yards from the hotel with Henry Robson. He told us that when they went to bed the first night of the storm, the stars were shining. In the night he heard it raining; and when they waked in the morning, the blizzard was in full blast with snow so blinding they could not tell the falling snow from the drifts. They reached the hotel with great difficulty and found it unusually crowded, mostly with stranded railroad crews.

All the guests slept upstairs in one huge room without partitions, some on cots, some on the floor. One corner was curtained off around two beds; this was known as "the Bridal Chamber" and was given to us. It was fun listening to the men playing pranks on each other and making remarks such as, "I can't find my pillow; oh, here it is in my ear."

It was two or three days before we got ourselves and our possessions moved out to the claim. Near the house was a small shanty and, a little farther on, another one to house a cow, but the cow was not bought until the next summer. There was no well, but the blizzard left great drifts of clean, white snow which stayed all winter. By melting this snow and keeping it in a barrel in a corner of the room, we were supplied with water.

We had brought along our wood-burning cookstove and a small heater good for burning wood or coal. Mother had bought what she considered a fair supply of non-perishable provisions—potatoes, preserved fruits, a half hog salted down, a large jar of lard and garden seeds for next

year's planting. It never occurred to her that we might be shut off from fuel and food for several months that winter. The stores in town carried only small stocks, so when after Christmas the railroad gave up trying to keep the track open, those supplies were soon exhausted.

When pioneers get together, the question always arises, "How did you live during the 'Hard Winter'?" Well, no one starved; neither was there high living for anyone and no use trying to pretend. One lady bragged they had put in such ample supplies they were living very well, but her little girl spoiled it when she piped up with "Taters and salt is my best holt" [her meaning is obscure].

When pioneers get together, the question always arises, "How did you live during the 'Hard Winter'?"

Fortunately for us our nearest neighbors, the Boasts, had come a year earlier and had raised some wheat; so when our flour gave out, we got a little wheat from them, ground it in their large coffee mill, and made it into muffins or used it as breakfast food with sugar syrup. Sometimes a boy would come on horseback from the Lake Henry settlement, a couple of miles southeast, to sell us a pound or two of butter and sometimes a little buttermilk. Dad would walk to town once in a while and pick up what food he could find. Sometimes two or three men would take a large hand sled and walk east on the railroad track until they reached a town where they could buy a few provisions and pick up the mail. These provisions were carefully parceled out so every family got a share, maybe only five pounds of flour.

Fuel was a problem. Having intended to buy a cow, Dad had cut some hay in the little meadow near the house. He had left it piled in cocks, but after the storm it was covered deep with snow. By tapping on the crust of the snow, he could locate the cocks, dig down to them, then pile what he needed on a big sled made from leftover scraps of lumber, haul it to the house and dump it inside. We all fell to and twisted it to use to keep the fire

going. Hay does not hold heat very long so the house got mighty cold at night while we lay shivering and shuddering as we listened to the weird howling of the coyotes.

Mother and we children were seldom out of the house all that winter. The snow was so deep it was like living in a basement, and we children helped father cut steps in the snow so we could climb out. Little brother Marshall, five that winter, helped Dad nail the laths to the studding. He would pound five or six nails into each end as far up as he could reach. Marsh made a toy wagon from a cigar box with spools for wheels. Dad carved us monkeys on a stick with jointed arms and legs that, by the clever manipulation of a string, would climb up and down the stick. He made little wooden guns that, by means of a ramrod and a rubber band, would shoot paper wads.

I had my doll to care for; I never had but one and she was very precious. Dad made a little cradle for her out of laths. Marsh and I played train with turned-over chairs and with quilting frames for rails. We had marbles and dominoes, clothespins, and building blocks. Mother started me on my school work, to be continued during the next five years. In the evening, Dad would get out his old fiddle and play "Arkansas Traveler," "Monie Musk," and "Pop Goes the Weasel"; Mother taught us the songs. That is how we survived the Hard Winter.

OLD-TIME AMUSEMENTS

Along with the chill cold winds of approaching winter came the tumble weeds—"the tumbling, tumble weeds"—looking for all the world like a flock of rather dirty sheep running before the wind, the never-ceasing wind: inescapable, depressing, maddening. Then, once more, winter—staying

indoors; learning to do housework, to knit and to sew; paying closer attention to lessons; reading over our few books and reading the newspapers aloud. We subscribed to the *Kingsbury County News* and the *St. Paul Pioneer Press.*

We sang "The Little Old Sod Shanty on the Claim" to the tune of "Log Cabin in the Lane." The refrain went like this:

> The hinges were of leather, the windows had no glass;
> The board roof let the howling blizzard in;
> I could hear hungry coyotes as they crept up through the grass,
> In my little old sod shanty on the claim.

Nice people were settling the prairie around De Smet, but most were so far away we seldom visited them. Occasionally a child came to play with us but usually we played by ourselves, determined our own activities, thought our own thoughts, dreamed our own dreams. We never played with a gang; we knew nothing about working in a group. This way of living fosters individualism.

Our school district, No. 32, was organized and a schoolhouse built in 1881 on the Amos Whiting claim at Old Kingsbury, the beginning of a town that never materialized. It was on the railroad about two miles east of us. We attended that school for a few weeks with Jenny Ros (later Jenny Wheat) for our teacher. I don't know why we dropped out after that short period. There were some eleven children in the district.

One winter a group of young people asked to have a party at our

house, probably because Dad could supply the music. There were about a dozen of them and where they came from, I never knew. I think they danced a few square dances, but they seemed to prefer games. Not many of these games are popular now so I shall make note of them. Of course, there was Drop the Handkerchief, which will no doubt last forever; then there was London Bridge:

> London bridge is falling down, falling down, falling
> down;
> London bridge is falling down, my fair lady.

and The Miller:

> Happy is the miller who lives by himself;
> While the wheel turns 'round, he's gaining on his wealth;
> One hand in the hopper while the other holds the bag;
> As the wheel turns 'round, he cries out, "grab."

and The Mill Pond (someone stands in the middle of a circle, say it's someone named Gaylord, and everyone sings):

> Gaylord's in the millpond, he can't swim,
> How will he get out again?
> I don't know and I don't care
> For he hasn't got any true love there.
> Bow to the east, bow to the west;

Bow to the one that you love best.
If she ain't here just do your part;
And choose another with all your heart.

(he pulls a girl into the circle; they sing):

I advise tourists not to seek out Silver Lake. Better keep your sentimental picture of it as given by Laura.

O what a horrid choice you've made,
You could have done better if you hadn't been afraid;
Kiss her quickly and send her away,
And tell her you'll call some other day.

LAURA INGALLS WILDER

Laura Ingalls was born in Wisconsin, 1867. . . . To seek a new home, the family set out in a covered wagon, living for a time in Missouri, Indian Territory, Kansas, Nebraska, Minnesota, and finally settling on a claim near De Smet, Dakota Territory, on the shore of Silver Lake in 1877 or 1878 [1879]. Mr. Ingalls traveled with his wife and four daughters: Laura, then about ten years old; Mary, who was blind; and Carrie and Grace. (I advise tourists not to seek out Silver Lake. Better keep your sentimental picture of it as given by Laura. It was first thought to be a likely place for a slaughter house, and for years was used as a city dump; now it is nearly filled up.)

The family spent summers on the claim and winters in town. I think Mr. Ingalls was timekeeper for the C&NW Railroad, then under construction. I knew the family quite well, especially Carrie. Laura was about sixteen and finishing her last year of school when I arrived. Schools were not graded

then, but she was in about the eighth grade. She was fortunate in having for a teacher Professor V. S. L. Owen who gave pupils thorough instruction in the basic subjects. He recognized Laura's talent for writing and advised her to keep on with it, but she did not do so until she was about sixty-five years old. As a girl Laura was a medium blond with large blue eyes. She could hardly have been called pretty, but there was such sparkle and life in her expression that she was very attractive.

After leaving school she taught for a short time and then married a neighbor farmer boy, Almanzo Wilder, known as "Manly." They lived for awhile near De Smet where their daughter, Rose, was born in 1887 [1886]. Mr. Wilder was very fond of horses and always drove a "spanking" team.

Laura and her husband soon developed a wanderlust. I expect that if they had lived today, they would have bought a trailer. As it was they followed in her father's footsteps and fitted out a covered wagon and set out to see the world. They tarried for a time in several states. In 1894, they finally came to rest at Mansfield, Missouri, in the northern part of the beautiful Ozarks where they lived the rest of their lives on a little farm. This is where she wrote her eight books, all about her own family homelife in the various places they had lived.

All the people she mentions are real people with their real names. Her first book was published in 1932 when she was sixty-five. These books are referred to as children's classics; no library is complete without them.

Laura took an active interest in community life and often wrote articles for farm papers. She outlived the rest of her family and died at the age of ninety. She had been a serene, contented, homeloving woman with a keen interest in the world as it passed by her door.

MOTHER

In conclusion I would say pioneering isn't hard on children; they take their life as a matter of course. It is not too hard on men who get about and make outside contacts, but it is tough on women. Dad worked hard all day at De Smet and walked the three miles there every morning and back every night. It was an achievement, and he was proud of his ability to do it.

But Mother's lot was to stay home all day with a couple of small children, hoe the garden, and wrestle with the fleet-footed Jersey cow. One day Mother got the cow's picket rope twisted about her ankle and was dragged several rods. But the monotony, the loneliness was the worst of it.

In all the five years we lived on the claim, she went to only one public entertainment, a dance at the Exchange Hotel. She seldom got off the place for even part of a day. If we had had a horse and buggy, she could have found something different to look at once in a while. If we had been building up a farm, getting stock about us, and making progress, she might have felt it worthwhile. As it was, it was like putting her, at twenty-eight, into prison for the five best years of her life. It must have taken a lot out of her, too, when I was sick for so long the first summer with what was undoubtedly a burst appendix and no doctor to be had. And she grieved over the death of her youngest brother back in Illinois of typhoid; she felt if she had been with him to nurse him, he might not have died.

The third year she had a felon on her finger. By that time Dr. Davies had come to town, a fine doctor and surgeon. He came out and lanced the felon, but she developed blood poisoning, no doubt from the linseed meal she borrowed from a neighbor to use as a poultice (this had been used previously by their hired man who had had an infected foot). Anyway, the infection had progressed so far by the time the doctor was called again that he had to amputate her forefinger at the second joint.

Mother regained her health but she lost her courage. She drifted into deep despondency with long spells of weeping. She continually talked to herself and kept saying she wished she were dead. I was so frightened I told her she couldn't die; she dared not leave Marsh and me all alone. She looked at me as though she had entirely forgotten who I was, sighed and said, bitterly, "No, I guess I can't even die."

Now, when people get in that condition today, they are said to be having a nervous breakdown and are sent away for a complete change of scene; but in pioneer days they were said to be having the "blues" and were left to fight it out by themselves as best they could.

Then the five years were finally at an end, and we moved to town in time to save Mother's sanity.

CHAPTER 3

Food for Thought: Recipes from the Founders of De Smet

This chapter contains authentic recipes from pioneers that Laura Ingalls Wilder or Ma and Pa and Mary and Carrie (later Mrs. David Swanzey) and Grace (later Mrs. Nate Dow) would have known.

The Bettmann Archive

A device for picking seeds out of fruit

The key word is *authentic*. Every effort has been made to take the original recipe, and using the imprecise measurements provided by yesteryear, make the recipe work to give the modern-day fan of Mrs. Wilder's writings a flavor of those older days. The Hines family kitchens, particularly the kitchens of my sister Jane and of my mother, Flossie, became experimental laboratories in an endeavor to find a way to make these recipes work using today's measurements. (If you want to try these recipes in their original, 1914 form, you can order the *Cream City Cook Book* from the Laura Ingalls Wilder Memorial Society, De Smet, South Dakota 57231.)

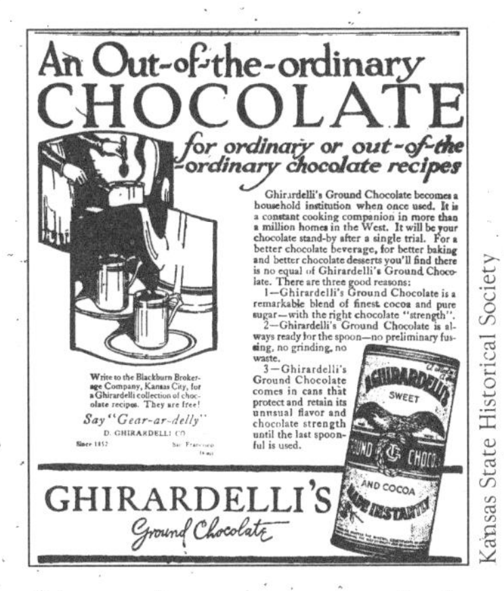

Kansas State Historical Society

Some products never go out of style.

Actually, a surprising number of the recipes needed little or no explanation or modification. Others, tried in various ways, have left us baffled. We'll warn you about the bafflers. Maybe, with warning, you will do better with them than we did.

Of course, it must ever be kept in mind

that these early pioneers may have expected different results from those we are used to now. If you make something and it turns out not to be quite up to your expectation, the same result might have been perfectly acceptable to the northern plainswoman who originally made the dish. Try these recipes as an experiment and for fun. SH

MRS. R. A. BOAST

First mentioned in By the Shores of Silver Lake, *Ella Boast and her husband, Rob, became steadfast friends of the Ingalls family. They were among the very first settlers in Kingsbury County, South Dakota, and they lived in and around De Smet, the Little Town on the Prairie, the rest of their lives. See chapter two, "Long Ago and Far Away," and appendix one for more about the Boasts.* SH

Nut Cake

½ cup butter
1½ cups sugar
3 eggs
2½ cups flour
½ cup milk
1 tablespoon baking powder
1 cup chopped nuts

Sift ½ cup of the flour with the baking powder and set aside.

Cream the butter and sugar until very light. Add the eggs and beat. Add the rest of the flour and milk and beat. Stir in the nuts.

Grease and flour a 9 × 13-inch baking pan. Heat oven to 350 degrees. Just before pouring batter into pan, stir in the sifted ½ cup flour and baking powder. Bake at 350 degrees for 25 to 30 minutes.

Ginger Cake

1 cup sugar
1 cup brown sugar dissolved in ½ cup hot water
⅔ cup butter or shortening
1 cup milk
2 eggs
1 teaspoon baking soda
1 teaspoon ginger
1 teaspoon cinnamon
1 teaspoon cloves
3 cups flour

Sift flour, soda, ginger, cinnamon, and cloves. Set aside.

Cream sugar and shortening. Add brown sugar mixture, eggs, and milk and mix. Stir in dry ingredients.

Pour into greased and floured 9 × 13-inch baking pan. Bake at 350 degrees for 35 to 40 minutes.

Doughnuts

1½ cups sugar
1 cup sour milk
2 eggs
2 tablespoons melted shortening
1 teaspoon baking soda
Pinch salt
⅛ teaspoon nutmeg
5½ cups flour

Make sour milk by placing 1 tablespoon lemon juice or vinegar in a measuring cup and filling to one cup with milk. Set aside a few minutes to sour.

Beat eggs. Add sugar, sour milk, melted shortening, soda, salt, and nutmeg and stir. Stir in flour to form a stiff, sticky dough. Toss lightly on a floured surface and roll out ½-inch thick. Cut with doughnut cutter.

Heat fat or vegetable oil 3 to 4 inches deep in heavy kettle (or deep-fat fryer) to 375 degrees. Fry doughnuts a few minutes on each side to a light golden brown.

MRS. F. C. BRADLEY

First mentioned in Little Town on the Prairie, *Mrs. Bradley was the druggist's wife. A cultured woman, Mrs. Bradley possessed an organ that was used for the town's "literaries," or entertainments. Mrs. Bradley's excellent singing brought tears to the eyes of Ma and Laura during one of the town's socials.* SH

Mrs. Bradley's singing brought tears to the eyes of Ma and Laura.

Steam Graham Loaf

- 1 cup molasses
- ½ cup sugar
- 2 cups sour milk
- 1 teaspoon salt
- ½ teaspoon baking powder
- 1 teaspoon baking soda, dissolved in 1 tablespoon boiling water
- ½ cup white flour
- 3 cups whole wheat flour

To make sour milk, place 2 tablespoons lemon juice in a quart measuring cup and add milk to make 2 cups. Set aside.

To make batter, mix ingredients in the order listed. Pour into four well-greased No. 2 cans. (Cans containing 20 ounces of fruit are usually No. 2 cans.) Fill cans two-thirds full or slightly less. Cover cans with double thickness of plastic wrap or waxed paper and fasten in place with rubber bands. The paper prevents steam that collects on the kettle's cover from falling onto the bread.

Place cans on a trivet in a deep kettle with a tight-fitting lid. (If you use a steamer, follow the manufacturer's directions.)

Pour boiling water to halfway up the sides of the cans or molds. Steam for two and one-half hours.

Remove the cans from the kettle and remove the paper from the top. Place the cans in a very hot oven (450 degrees) for 5 minutes. Cut out end of can with can opener and push out loaf. Slice with a heavy thread drawn around the loaf, crossing ends. Serve hot.

To reheat cooled or frozen bread, place it in a colander and cover with a clean dish towel. Steam 15 minutes over boiling water until hot.

(To heat frozen loaf in a microwave, unwrap bread and place on a plate. Cover with waxed paper. Microwave on 50% power for 6 to 8 minutes. Let stand 5 minutes before slicing.)

Cabbage Salad

- 4 cups chopped cabbage
- 1 bunch of celery, chopped
- 3 egg yolks
- 1 whole egg
- ½ cup sugar
- ⅔ cup vinegar
- 1 teaspoon dry mustard
- Pepper and salt to taste
- 1 cup sweet cream

Cook egg yolks, egg, sugar, vinegar, mustard, salt, and pepper until thick. Stir in cream. Pour hot dressing over cabbage and celery.

MRS. C. L. DAWLEY

The former Florence Garland was Laura's first teacher in De Smet and was Cap Garland's sister. Laura once admitted that, at first, she was more interested in Cap Garland than in Almanzo. Florence Dawley's husband was known to be one of the more outrageous practical jokers in De Smet. SH

Graham Gems

1 cup sour milk
½ cup sour cream
½ cup molasses
1 teaspoon soda
1 teaspoon salt
1½ cups whole wheat flour
¾ cup white flour

To make sour milk, place 1 tablespoon lemon juice or vinegar in a measuring cup and fill to one cup with milk. Let set 5 minutes.

Mix sour milk, sour cream, and molasses in small bowl. Combine dry ingredients in a mixing bowl. Add combined liquids all at once to dry ingredients. Mix only until all ingredients are moistened.

Fill greased muffin cups two-thirds full. Bake at 400 degrees for 20 to 25 minutes. Cool briefly in cups and then turn out on rack or towel.

(Note: There are no eggs or oil in this recipe.)

Black Chocolate Cake

½ cup cocoa
¾ cup and 2 tablespoons hot water
2 cups light brown sugar
½ cup butter
2 eggs
1 cup sour milk
1 teaspoon baking soda
1 teaspoon baking powder
2 cups flour

Dissolve cocoa in hot water. Set aside to cool.

Make sour milk by putting 1 tablespoon lemon juice or vinegar in a measuring cup and filling to one cup with milk. Set aside a few minutes to sour.

Cream butter, sugar, and eggs. Beat in dissolved cocoa.

Sift together flour, baking soda, and baking powder. Add to batter alternately with sour milk.

Pour into greased and floured 9 × 13-inch baking pan. Bake at 350 degrees for 30 to 35 minutes until toothpick inserted in center comes out clean and cake begins to pull away from edges of pan.

Apple Charlotte

Butter a deep baking dish. Cover bottom with a layer of sliced, peeled apples. Add a layer of stale, buttered bread crumbs, then a layer of apples sprinkled with sugar and a little cinnamon. Continue layering bread crumbs, apples, and sugar and cinnamon until dish is full, using apples for the top layer. Moisten with hot water and bake, covered, until apples are done (about 40 minutes at 350 degrees for a 9-inch loaf pan). Uncover and bake until browned, 10 minutes. Serve warm with sugar and cream.

Cranberry Pie

- 1¼ cups split cranberries
- 1¼ cups sugar
- 2 tablespoons flour
- Water
- 2-crust 9-inch pie shell

Measure cranberries and add water to measuring cup to cover cranberries. Combine sugar and flour in a mixing bowl and add cranberries. Pour into pie shell. Cover with top crust. Cut steam vents. Bake at 425 degrees for 30 to 40 minutes or until juice bubbles and crust is browned.

MRS. C. S. G. FULLER

Gerald Fuller and his hardware store are mentioned numerous times in The Long Winter *and* Little Town on the Prairie. *Mr. C. S. G. Fuller was*

a partner with Gerald in this store. Mrs. Fuller was active in the Congregational Church and community affairs. She crossed paths with the Ingalls family numerous times. Gerald Fuller used his clog dancing to good effect in a minstrel show in Little Town on the Prairie. SH

Rolls

4 cups milk
½ cup shortening
½ cup sugar
1 tablespoon salt
2 packages dry yeast
1 cup warm water
10 to 11 cups bread flour
½ cup melted butter or margarine

Scald milk and pour over shortening, sugar, and salt in a very large mixing bowl. Cool to room temperature. Dissolve yeast in water. (The water needs to be just warm enough to dissolve the yeast—lukewarm.) Add yeast to cooled milk. Add 6½ cups flour to make a stiff batter. Cover and let rise until doubled and bubbly, about 2 hours.

Stir down mixture and add enough flour to make a soft dough, 3 to 4 cups. Turn out on floured surface and knead 15 minutes. Clean bowl and grease lightly. Return dough to bowl, turning to grease top. Let rise until doubled, about 1½ hours.

Divide dough in half and roll to ½-inch thickness. Cut with 3″ round biscuit cutter. Brush with melted butter, fold over, and press to seal edges. Place on greased baking sheets.

Cover and let rise until doubled, about 30 minutes. Bake at 375 degrees for 12 to 15 minutes. Remove from baking sheet and brush tops with melted butter.

(Note: Because you set a sponge in this recipe by first making a prefermented smaller part of the larger dough, it is important not to start with your liquids too warm or your first rising will be too fast. Also, do not use quick-rise yeast. The high gluten in bread flour will also help your bread be light through all the risings. Mrs. Fuller said this recipe would make 4 dozen rolls. When we tested the recipe, it made 4 dozen rolls and a 9 x 13-inch pan of cinnamon rolls.)

White Cake

½ cup butter
1½ cups sugar
1 cup milk or water
2½ cups flour
2 teaspoons baking powder
5 egg whites
1½ cups chopped nuts (optional)

Sift the flour and baking powder and set aside.

Cream the butter and gradually add the sugar. Add the flour alternately with the milk. Beat the whole mixture for 5 minutes. Beat the egg whites until stiff and fold into the batter. Pour into two greased and floured 8-inch round cake pans or one 9 × 13-inch baking pan.

Bake at 350 degrees for 25 to 30 minutes. Cool 10 minutes. Turn out on cooling racks.

(Note: To make a nut cake, add 1½ cups chopped nuts before folding in the egg whites.)

Cucumber Pickles

2 gallons whole, small cucumbers
2 gallons water
4 cups pickling salt
½ cup white mustard seed
2 tablespoons whole allspice
2 tablespoons peppercorns
2 tablespoons whole cloves
¾ cup broken cinnamon sticks
3 red peppers, cut in chunks
A few pieces of fresh horseradish
2 cups brown sugar
1 cup molasses
6 cups vinegar

Dissolve pickling salt in water. Add cucumbers and soak for three days in stone crock, glass, pottery, or unchipped enamel-lined pan. Place a plate almost as large as the crock over the cucumbers and lay something heavy on top to keep cucumbers under the brine.

On the fourth day, rinse pickles well and wipe dry.

Tie the mustard seed, allspice, peppercorns, cloves, and cinnamon in a cloth bag. Boil the spices in 1 cup of vinegar, along with the red pepper and horseradish.

Add the spiced vinegar to the remaining vinegar and brown sugar and bring to a boil. Pour over cucumbers, adding more vinegar if needed to cover. Weigh down the cucumbers with a plate as before.

On each of days four through ten, drain off vinegar and scald. Pour again over cucumbers. Weigh down.

On the eleventh day, drain off vinegar and add 1 cup of molasses before scalding. Pack cucumbers in hot, sterilized glass jars. Pour hot syrup over cucumbers to cover. Seal. Process jars in boiling water bath (212 degrees F.) for 5 minutes.

Cream Pie

1½ cups half-and-half
2 egg yolks (save whites for meringue)
½ cup sugar
2 teaspoons cornstarch
1 teaspoon vanilla
1 baked 8-inch pie shell

Heat half-and-half in top of double boiler. Combine egg yolks, sugar, and cornstarch. Add to half-and-half. Cook, stirring constantly, until thick and smooth. Remove from heat. Add vanilla. Stir until smooth and blended. Pour hot filling into pie shell.

Beat egg whites until stiff, gradually adding 2 tablespoons sugar. Heap on top of pie. Place in 350 degree oven to brown for 10 to 15 minutes.

MRS. F. L. HARTHORN

The Harthorns were a prominent De Smet family, and Harthorn's Dry Goods store was one of the earliest businesses in De Smet. The Harthorns were among the band of approximately eighty families that endured the "long winter" together. The Harthorn store was less than half a block from Pa Ingalls's house on Second Street. SH

Pop Corn Balls

3 gallons popped corn
2 cups sugar
1 cup water
½ teaspoon cream of tartar

Sort out any unpopped kernels and place popped corn in a very large container. Boil sugar, water, and cream of tartar to hard ball stage (250 to 266 degrees on a candy thermometer).

Pour syrup over popped corn, stirring quickly to coat. Make into balls as fast as possible, keeping hands moist by dipping them often in cold water.

(Note: While the syrup did not coat this amount of popcorn well, it did coat it enough to be able to form the mixture into balls. You might want to add 1 teaspoon vanilla to the syrup for flavoring.)

French Cream Cake

1 cup sugar
3 eggs, separated
1½ cups flour
1 teaspoon baking powder
4 tablespoons water
1 teaspoon vanilla

Beat egg yolks and sugar. Add flour, baking powder, water, and vanilla. Beat egg whites until stiff and fold into batter. Bake in greased and floured loaf pan at 350 degrees for 40 to 45 minutes.

(Note: The original instructions said to bake in a loaf pan or three layer pans. The recipe did not make enough batter to fill two layer pans. The ingredients did not include shortening, so the cake was very dry and tough. Good luck!)

It is fitting that this brave but retiring lady would not draw attention to herself.

MRS. C. P. INGALLS

Caroline Lake Quinter Ingalls, Laura Ingalls Wilder's mother, is represented here by a single recipe. Somehow it is fitting that this brave but retiring lady would not draw attention to herself even though she was a fine cook, and fine cooking was one of the few ways a woman could draw attention to herself during those pioneer days. Her husband, Charles Philip, was the first Justice of the Peace of De Smet and "Pa" to all fans of the books. SH

Mixed Pickles

- 1 gallon chopped cabbage
- 1 gallon green tomatoes
- 1 quart onions
- 3 green peppers
- ½ cup pickling salt
- 4 tablespoons ground mustard seed
- 2 tablespoons ginger
- 1 tablespoon cloves
- 1 tablespoon cinnamon
- 1 tablespoon allspice
- 6 cups sugar
- 1 ounce celery seed
- 6 cups vinegar

Chop cabbage, tomatoes, onions, and peppers; sprinkle with salt and let stand an hour or two; press out water.

Mix in other spices, sugar, and celery seed and 6 cups of vinegar or enough to cover the vegetables. Boil slowly for 20 minutes.

Pour into hot, sterilized glass jars. Seal. Process in boiling water bath (212 degrees F.) for 5 minutes.

MRS. D. H. LOFTUS

Mr. Loftus was another of the general merchants of De Smet. His attempt to reap a generous profit on wheat brought into the winter-beseiged prairie town during the "long winter" became a dramatic show-down in Laura's book of that title. Mrs. Loftus kept to her cooking. SH

White Layer Cake

4 egg whites, beaten very stiff
1 cup sugar
½ cup milk
½ cup butter
1 teaspoon baking soda
1 teaspoon cream of tartar
1½ cups flour

Sift flour, soda, and cream of tartar. Set aside.

Cream butter and sugar. Add milk and beat. Add the egg whites and sifted flour and beat 3 minutes.

Pour batter into greased and floured 9 × 13-inch pan or two 8-inch round cake pans. Bake for 15 to 20 minutes at 350 degrees.

(Note: This cake was put together following the directions Mrs. Loftus provided in the recipe. All the air beaten into the egg whites was, of course, beaten out in the 3 minutes at the end. It made a quite thin 9 × 13-inch cake. One wonders if the egg whites should not have been folded in *after* the flour was beaten into the batter. Try that for better results.)

Sea Foam Candy

2 cups brown sugar
½ cup water
1 egg white
1 teaspoon vanilla
½ cup chopped nuts

Boil brown sugar and water to the soft ball stage (235 to 240 degrees on a candy thermometer).

Stiffly beat the egg white. Pour the boiling syrup on the egg white in a steady stream, continuing to beat constantly. When it gets a little stiff, add the vanilla and chopped nuts.

When the mixture will stand alone, drop by rounded spoonfuls on waxed paper or a buttered pan. Store tightly covered.

Peach and Orange Conserve

12 peaches
6 oranges
2 cups water
2 cups blanched almonds, chopped
7 cups sugar

Peel and cut up peaches. Grate the rind from the oranges, using none of the white. Cut the pulp into slices.

Cook peaches, oranges, grated rind, sugar and water until thick and clear, adding almonds the last 15 minutes. Pour into hot jars; seal. Makes 10 small glasses.

Gooseberry Conserve

6 quarts gooseberries
6 oranges
4 cups raisins
24 cups sugar

Grind gooseberries and oranges (rind and all). Add raisins and sugar. Stir to combine. Bring mixture to a boil. Cook over low heat, stirring frequently, until thick. Pour into hot jars; seal.

Doughnuts

⅔ cup sugar
4 tablespoons melted butter
2 eggs
1 cup buttermilk
1 teaspoon baking soda
1 teaspoon cinnamon
⅛ teaspoon nutmeg
3½ cups flour

Sift soda, cinnamon, nutmeg, and flour together. Set aside.

Beat sugar, melted butter, and eggs. Add buttermilk. Add dry ingredients all at once, stirring only to moisten dry ingredients.

Heat shortening or salad oil 3 to 4 inches deep in heavy kettle (or deep-fat fryer to 375 degrees.)

Using two spoons (dipped in hot fat to keep dough from sticking), drop dough in small rounded tablespoonfuls into fat, using other spoon to push the dough off the spoon. Fry 3 to 4 minutes to a golden brown. (Most of the doughnuts will turn themselves over when cooked on one side, but you may have to give some of them a little help.)

Lift doughnuts from fat with a slotted spoon and drain on paper towels. Roll hot doughnuts in granulated sugar.

Pudding

1¼ cups fine dry bread crumbs
2 cups flour
1 cup suet, chopped fine
1 cup raisins
1 cup molasses
1 cup milk
1 tablespoon soda
1 teaspoon salt
1 teaspoon cloves
1 teaspoon cinnamon

Combine all ingredients. Pour into well-oiled 2-quart mold. Cover securely with mold lid or several thicknesses of waxed paper tied in place with string.

Place mold on a rack in covered kettle of boiling water. (Water should come halfway up on the mold.) Steam on low heat for 3 hours. Unmold pudding onto serving plate.

Mrs. Tinkham held the first "dime sociable" in De Smet.

Lemon Pie

1 cup sugar
2 tablespoons cornstarch
Juice and grated rind of
 1 lemon (2 tablespoons juice, 1 teaspoon lemon zest)
3 tablespoons butter
 (butter the size of an egg)
1 cup hot water
1 egg, separated
2 tablespoons sugar
1 8-inch pie shell

Combine sugar, cornstarch, lemon juice, rind, butter, and hot water in saucepan. Cook until clear. Remove from heat and put a little of the hot pudding into a mixing bowl with a beaten egg yolk. Stir and return to saucepan; return pan to heat and cook to boiling. Cool.

Make meringue by beating egg white until stiff and gradually adding 2 tablespoons sugar. Pour pudding into baked shallow 8-inch pie shell. Top with meringue. Bake at 350 degrees until brown for 10 to 15 minutes.

(Note: The filling needs another tablespoon of cornstarch and another egg yolk to make it thicken. The pie made using the directions above could have been eaten with a straw. It was very sweet and probably could have used twice the lemon juice.)

MRS. C. H. TINKHAM

Tinkham's furniture store was an early De Smet business. Mrs. Tinkham had the distinction of holding the first "dime sociable," one of the first gatherings to spark the town's social life as recorded in Little Town on the Prairie. *The Tinkham store was in the same block and across the street from the Ingallses' home.* SH

Brown Bread

3 cups whole wheat flour
2 cups milk, sweet or sour
1 cup molasses
½ cup raisins
2 teaspoons baking soda, dissolved in 2 tablespoons boiling water

Combine all ingredients. Pour into four well-greased No. 2 cans. (No. 2 cans hold 20 ounces of fruit.)

Steam 3 hours. (See notes included with Steam Graham Loaf of Mrs. F. C. Bradley, page 40.)

Cocoa Frosting

4 teaspoons cocoa
2 tablespoons cold water
3 tablespoons hot water
1 teaspoon vanilla
Speck of salt
1¾ cups confectioner's sugar

Put cocoa in saucepan; add cold water and stir until smooth. Add hot water and cook for one to two minutes; add vanilla and salt. Stir in sugar and beat until smooth and glossy, adding a little more water if too thick or more sugar if too thin.

(Note: To get a frosting thick enough to spread, we used 3½ cups powdered sugar, but doing so overpowered the chocolate so that we couldn't taste it.)

Baked Bean Soup

1 cup baked beans
1 cup cold water
1 onion
1 cup tomatoes
1 cup milk
1 tablespoon butter
1 tablespoon flour
Pepper and salt to taste
Chopped celery

Cook beans, water, onion, and tomatoes until soft. (Strain or puree in food processor.) Add milk, butter, and flour to thicken soup. Season to taste and serve sprinkled with chopped celery.

MRS. D. W. WILMARTH

The Wilmarths were early settlers of De Smet too. After 1883 they were a prominent part of town life. In company with his brother George, D. W. ran a grocery that was still in business when old settlers celebrated the fiftieth anniversary of the town. Laura and Almanzo would have known the Wilmarths because they didn't leave De Smet for good until 1894. SH

Lemon Filling

1 egg
1 cup white sugar
1 tablespoon butter
1 tablespoon cornstarch
½ cup water
1 teaspoon grated lemon rind
2 tablespoons lemon juice

Combine all ingredients in a heavy saucepan. Bring to a boil, stirring constantly. Cool, stirring occasionally.

Black Chocolate Cake

3 eggs, separated
1¼ cups sugar
1 cup sour cream, divided
1 cup flour
4 (1 ounce) squares unsweetened chocolate
1 teaspoon vanilla
1 teaspoon baking soda dissolved in 1 tablespoon boiling water

Melt chocolate and ½ cup sour cream. Set aside.

Beat egg yolks, sugar, and remaining ½ cup sour cream. Stir in flour. Add chocolate and vanilla.

Fold in stiffly beaten egg whites. Dissolve baking soda in boiling water. Stir into batter.

Pour into greased and floured 9 × 13-inch baking pan. Bake at 350 degrees for 15 to 20 minutes.

(Note: There is no butter or shortening in this cake. The sour cream supplies the butterfat in this recipe.

The batter was rather thick before adding the egg whites so most of the air is lost when you fold the whites in. This makes a rather thin, fudgy cake.

This cake was made once using commercial sour cream and again using whipping cream soured with 1 tablespoon of lemon juice. Either way, the melted chocolate and sour cream became very thick making it difficult to completely melt the chocolate without burning the mixture. It might work better to melt the chocolate and then stir in the sour cream.)

Boiled Icing

1 cup sugar
½ cup water
1 egg white
¼ teaspoon cream of tartar
1 teaspoon lemon juice

Boil sugar and water together until it spins a thread (230 to 233 degrees on a candy thermometer). Beat the egg white and cream of tartar to a stiff froth. Add the syrup in a steady stream, beating constantly. Flavor with the lemon juice. Beat until cold. Spread on cooled cake.

(Note: When this recipe was tested and cooked until the syrup would spin a thread, the result was a very dry, divinity-like mixture that would not spread.)

Cream Puffs

1 cup water
½ cup butter
1 cup flour
3 unbeaten eggs

Melt butter in water and bring to a rolling boil. Add flour all at once and stir vigorously until mixture forms a ball that does not separate—30 seconds to 1 minute. Remove from heat and cool for 10 minutes.

Add eggs one at a time, beating about 1 minute or until mixture is smooth again.

Drop dough in rounded tablespoons on greased baking sheet. Bake at 400 degrees for 20 to 30 minutes until golden brown. Puffs should sound hollow when tapped with finger. Remove puffs from baking sheet and cool on wire rack. When cool, fill with whipped cream.

(Note: Most modern-day recipes for cream puffs recommend using 4 eggs. The additional egg creates more steam in the baking process, resulting in a cream puff that is hollower with less eggy dough that needs to be pulled out before filling the puff.)

Pineapple Sherbet

6 cups water
2 cups sugar
Juice of 3 lemons (6 tablespoons)
20-ounce can crushed pineapple, undrained
1 egg white

Simmer water and sugar together to dissolve sugar. Cool.

Puree pineapple in blender or food processor. Add pineapple and lemon juice to syrup. Freeze in an ice cream freezer. If using an electric freezer, this will take about 20 minutes.

Beat the egg white. Whisk into sherbet.

MRS. WHALEY

When Neva Whaley Harding was one hundred years old, some friends gathered some of her writings and speeches about old Dakota days. The Ingallses, particularly Carrie and Laura, are prominent in her memory. This recipe is her mother's. In chapter two, you read of Mrs. Whaley's battle against loneliness and depression on a homestead. One has to wonder if Ma Ingalls ever felt overwhelmed by such feelings as she tried to raise a family without the benefit of nearby neighbors or relatives. SH

Strawberry Sherbet

1 quart strawberries, stems and hulls removed
2 cups sugar
4 cups water
2 tablespoons strawberry gelatin (optional)
Juice of 1 lemon (2 tablespoons)
2 egg whites
2 tablespoons sugar

Simmer 2 cups sugar, water, and gelatin to dissolve sugar. Cool.

Mash strawberries. Strain by working through colander (or puree in food processor). Add strawberries to syrup, along with lemon juice. Freeze in an ice cream freezer. If using an electric freezer, this will take about 20 minutes.

Beat the egg whites until frothy and gradually add 2 tablespoons sugar. Beat until stiff peaks form. Whisk into the finished sherbet.

Part 3

Reminiscences of Laura's Life in Mansfield, Missouri

CHAPTER 4

Celebrated Author: The Mansfield Era

Mrs. Wilder's fame has always bewildered her adopted town of Mansfield. She lived as a farmer's wife and an active rural neighbor to the town for almost forty years before writing a published book under the name Laura Ingalls Wilder.

By the time she did this radical thing—writing a book—her daughter, Rose, was the town's famous cosmopolitan citizen, a world traveler who had eschewed further voyages to return to her native village—population approximately eight hundred—to write. The town recognized Mrs. Wilder as a former correspondent for the *Missouri Ruralist*. But by her late fifties she had given up even that modest task, and the Wilders were supposedly in retirement. Thus, it took Mansfield many years to become reconciled to Mrs. Wilder's latter-day fame as a famous storyteller. Indeed, most people you talk to will begin with an apology: "If I had only known that she would become famous, I would have paid more attention to what she said and did."

Her daughter, Rose, was the town's famous cosmopolitan citizen.

Certainly people in Mansfield had little idea of the importance of her books, as you can see from the following artless, but appreciative, book review of *Little House on the Prairie*, which appeared in her local paper on October 3, 1935. Surely it must have delighted as well as amused Mrs. Wilder:

> Mrs. Laura Ingalls Wilder have our thanks for a copy of her very latest book, "The Little House on the Prairie." The book has been read, every word and a very interesting book it is.
>
> It goes back to her childhood life of pioneer days when she left the "Little House in the Woods," in Wisconsin, with her parents, in a covered wagon and came to the Kansas plains where

they built their little house and started life anew, only to last a year at that place.

From the very beginning of the book, every paragraph is so absorbing till one loses sight of the present time and drifts back to the plain and meager way of living and all of which was happy. One pictures in their mind each character which were Pa and Ma, Mary, Laura and baby Carrie. Their constant and ever faithful watch dog and their good mustang ponies, Pet and Patty.

Every chapter has a thrill. How they built their little house, the children playing round the door, the chimney catching on fire when Pa was away one windy day, the wolves howling, Indians on a war dance that lasted for a week, and a number of other exciting things.

The book holds the interest of the reader till one becomes in mind. A character of it. Living simple and happy in God's great universe. We read this book evenings. Retire and our minds run on, of the real experiences of this happy little family of many years ago.

Mrs. Wilder's book, "Farmer Boy," which was published more than a year ago was adopted as a text book in many schools. We have not read this book but understand it is one of the most interesting. We are indeed very proud of the book. You know some writer one time said, "A good friend to books, is a good friend to have."

This ending quote, "A good friend to books, is a good friend to have," sums up Mansfield's impression of Laura Ingalls Wilder.

The people of Mansfield, Missouri, claimed Laura as their own. And they claimed some credit for influencing her life. Debbie Von Behren, award-winning teacher, native of the town, and freelance writer, summarized this feeling in a volume called *Mansfield: First One Hundred Years* (her full article is reprinted in appendix two):

> We aren't the only town in America to claim Laura Ingalls Wilder for our own. Every community she has lived in wants some of the glory of having had a famous citizen. Well, I hate to disappoint them, but I think Laura especially belongs to Mansfield. She and Almanzo chose our town, she lived here for over 60 years, and most important, she wrote every single one of her books here.
>
> We know Laura was special. But there also has to be something special about the town that provided the environment necessary for her talent to shine through.

Certainly Mansfield has its place in any reminiscence of Laura Ingalls Wilder. A quick look at the events that occurred during the sixty years Laura lived here shows how important this era of her life was to her writing career:

1894	Laura and Almanzo purchase Rocky Ridge Farm.
1911	Laura starts to write for the *Missouri Ruralist.*
1932	Laura's first book, *Little House in the Big Woods,* is published.
1933	*Farmer Boy* published.
1935	*Little House on the Prairie* published.
1937	*On the Banks of Plum Creek* published.

1940	*The Long Winter* published.
1943	*Little Town on the Prairie* and *These Happy Golden Years* published. (Wilder's books are available from HarperCollins Publishers.)
1947	Garth Williams, illustrator of such books as *Stuart Little*, retraces the Ingallses' journeys as he works on illustrating a new edition of the books.
October 23, 1949	Almanzo Wilder dies at age 92 and is buried in Mansfield.
February 10, 1957	Laura Ingalls Wilder dies at age 90, three days after her birthday, and is buried in Mansfield.

The Mansfield years tell us a great deal about who Laura was and how she lived. I begin part three of this book with interviews and feature articles about the Wilders' lives from the Mansfield paper, the *Mansfield Mirror*, and the *Missouri Ruralist*, a biweekly journal for Missouri farmers and breeders. Next are personal reminiscences of friends and neighbors—Neta Seal, Nava Austin, Irene V. Lichty, and the Jones family.

In this section of the book, as in the first and second sections, Laura speaks for herself in articles she published in the *Missouri Ruralist*: first her reflections on World War I and then her reports of the various activities of the women's clubs in Mansfield along with her thoughts on women's choices in the 1920s.

When Laura first began writing her column, "The Farm Home," for the *Missouri Ruralist*, John F. Case, editor of the newspaper, introduced her in this way: "We always have known that the women and girls are about the most important folks on the farm, but sometimes the editor, being a man, forgets to give them their rightful due in columns of space. Right now we promise to be more liberal. Mrs. A. J. Wilder, long connected with this paper,

Herbert Hoover Presidential Library

Mrs. Laura Ingalls Wilder at the height of her writing career

and one of the most versatile writers contributing to the farm press, is to pay you a neighborly visit every two weeks. Mrs. Wilder lives on a farm and she not only knows but feels the things she writes about. Watch for Mrs. Wilder's paragraphs; they will surely interest you."

Recently the relationship between Laura and her daughter, Rose, has come under great scrutiny. Did Rose edit or rewrite her mother's books? What was the relationship between them like? Chapter eleven looks at their relationship from the eyes of people who knew them both. I end part three with a potpourri of reminiscences.

Let's begin these Mansfield years now with an article that introduced readers to Laura as one of the columnists of the *Missouri Ruralist*: "Let's Visit Mrs. Wilder," the fifth article in the *Ruralist*'s "Get Acquainted" series. SH

Let's Visit Mrs. Wilder

INTERVIEW IN THE *MISSOURI RURALIST*
February 20, 1918
By John F. Case

"I was a regular little tomboy."

Laura Ingalls Wilder had written regularly for the Missouri Ruralist *since 1916. Mr. John Case, the editor of the* Ruralist, *saw Mrs. Wilder's talent and unique observations and wanted to further her career—and the influence of the* Ruralist *among women. Mr. Case can truly be said to be the first significant journalist to recognize Laura's talent. He also noted that by the age of fifty she had already led a full life. Yet it would be fifteen more years before her first book would be published to wide acclaim! Mr. Case had no idea what he was starting.* SH

"I was born in a log house within four miles of the legend-haunted Lake Pepin in Wisconsin," Mrs. Wilder wrote when I asked for information about her. "I remember seeing deer that father had killed hanging in the trees about our forest home. When I was four years old, we traveled to the Indian Territory—Fort Scott, Kansas, being our nearest town. My childish memories hold the sound of the war whoop, and I see pictures of painted Indians."

Looking at the picture of Mrs. Wilder, which was recently taken, we find it difficult to believe that she is old enough to be the pioneer described. But having confided her age to the editor (not for publication), we must be convinced that it is true. Surely Mrs. Wilder, who is the mother of Rose Wilder Lane, talented author and writer, has found the fountain of youth in

Courtesy of Nava Austin

Laura in her late sixties

the Ozark hills. We may well believe that she has a "cheerful disposition" as her friend asserts.

"I was a regular little tomboy," Mrs. Wilder confesses, "and it was fun to walk the two miles to school." The folks were living in Minnesota then, but it was not long until Father Ingalls, who seems to have had a penchant for moving about, had located in Dakota. It was at De Smet, South Dakota, that Laura Ingalls, then eighteen years old, married A. J. Wilder, a farmer boy. "Our daughter, Rose Wilder Lane, was born on the farm," Mrs. Wilder informs us, "and it was there I learned to do all kinds of farm work with machinery. I have ridden the binder, driving six horses. And I could ride. I do not wish to appear conceited, but I broke my own ponies to ride. Of course, they were not bad, but they were broncos." Mrs. Wilder had the spirit that brought success to the pioneers.

Mr. Wilder's health failed and the Wilders went to Florida. "I was something of a curiosity, being the only 'Yankee girl' the inhabitants ever had seen," Mrs. Wilder relates. The low altitude did not agree with Mrs.

Wilder, though, and she became ill. It was then that they came to Rocky Ridge Farm near Mansfield, Wright County [Missouri], and there they have lived for twenty-five years. Only forty acres were purchased, and the land was all timber except a four-acre, worn-out field. "Illness and traveling expenses had taken our surplus cash, and we lacked $150 of paying for the forty acres," Mrs. Wilder writes. "Mr. Wilder was unable to do a full day's work. The garden, my hens, and the wood I helped saw and which we sold in town took us through the first year. It was then I became an expert at the end of a cross-cut saw, and I still can 'make a hand' in an emergency. Mr. Wilder says he would rather have me help than any man he ever sawed with. And, believe me, I learned how to take care of hens and to make them lay."

One may wonder that so busy a person, as Mrs. Wilder has proved to be, can find time to write. "I always have been a busy person," she says, "doing my own housework, helping the Man of the Place when help could not be obtained; but I love to work. And it is a pleasure to write. And, oh, I do just love to play! The days never have been long enough to do the things I would like to do. Every year has held more of interest than the year before." Folks who possess that kind of spirit get a lot of joy out of life as they travel the long road.

JOINED THE FAMILY IN 1911

Mrs. Wilder has held numerous important offices, and her stories about farm life and farm folks have appeared in the best farm papers. Her first article printed [for us] appeared in February 1911. It was a copy of an address prepared for Farmer's Week. So for seven years she has been talking to Missouri women through these columns, talk that always has carried inspiration and incentive for worthwhile work.

Reading Mrs. Wilder's contributions, most folks doubtless have decided that she is a college graduate. But "my education has been what a girl would get on the frontier," she informs us. "I never graduated from anything and only attended high school two terms."

Folks who know Mrs. Wilder, though, know that she is a cultured, well-educated gentlewoman. Combined with inherent ability, unceasing study of books has provided the necessary education, and greater things have been learned from the study of life itself.

Mrs. Wilder Led Hard Life in Setting Up Home

INTERVIEW IN THE MANSFIELD MIRROR
May 2, 1957

Mrs. Laura Ingalls Wilder's death on February 10, 1957, only three days after her ninetieth birthday was a seemingly small event. The big news of the day was who would succeed Eisenhower as president. Were the Russians gaining on us in science and math? Were we getting behind in the arms race?

Up the road from Mansfield, Mrs. Wilder was just the neighbor who lived about a mile from town. She had been there forever and bothered nobody. Sure, sometimes she would get a few hundred cards for her birthday, sometimes nearly a thousand, but who could account for that? Celebrity *was the last word you'd ever use about Mrs. Wilder. She herself had finished the story of her life in* These Happy Golden Years. *At the end of the story she was only eighteen and newly married to Almanzo Wilder, a farmer.*

Then came her death.

Naturally, Mansfield knew there would be some curiosity, but a New York Times *obituary was surprising. Then the letters started coming. "Could you send us a copy of the* Mansfield Mirror *obituary?" "What more can you tell us about Mrs. Wilder? We feel like we have lost a personal friend." The ordinary farm woman who lived just up the road wasn't so ordinary.*

Mansfield tried to cope with the deluge of inquiry. A few months

after Mrs. Wilder's death, as the idea spread for the creation of a memorial to Mrs. Wilder that would preserve her home as a museum, the newspaper took it upon itself to feature the town's most famous citizen in a full front-page tribute.

The following piece is a reprint of an interview Mrs. Wilder gave a St. Louis reporter a few years before her death. This article appeared with other articles on the front page of the May 2, 1957, issue of the Mirror *as a memorial to Laura, their local celebrity who had died only three months before. Some of the other articles were:*

- *"Wilder's Home Just Like Topsy" (the next article in this section of the book)*
- *"Mrs. Wilder's Pen Is Stilled at Age of 90 Years" (reprinted in appendix two)*
- *"Citizens Form Group to Get Court Charter"* SH

Mrs. Almanzo Wilder, with silvery white hair, sits and plays solitaire or crochets in her Ozark mountain home, daintily dressed in a black dress with white lace collar. She is 84 years old, but her eyes snap with vitality and kindly humor. She looks fragile and even in her prime must have been delicately built. Yet she had led a life of hard labor, felling trees, tilling soil, tending poultry and livestock. She has survived a childhood spent in the northern wilderness and in claim shanties of Dakota Territory.

She learned Indian omens from the Indians themselves and by observing learned of the bitter struggle for survival by animals of woods and prairie. She traveled by covered wagon and cooked on the trail. When she was so small that she had to stand on a dry goods box to work at the kitchen table, she helped make soap and hominy, kneaded bread and made cambric tea.

It was during the "Long Winter" when Laura's family was snow-bound from October to May, 60 miles from any shipping center. No trains came until May. Her writings tell of their existence during this time.

The books began with her life in the Wisconsin woods and follow in sequence the various moves of her family to the Dakota prairie in Minnesota, Dakota Territory, and to another claim shanty in Indian Territory, now Oklahoma.

The authoress went on to tell, "Almanzo Wilder and I were married in Dakota Territory and when Rose (the daughter) was 7, we came in a covered wagon to this farm. We brought all our belongings —one bed spring, a feather mattress, piece-work quilts, pots and pans, a skillet, coffee pot and a little homemade cupboard. We bought 200 acres of these beautiful hills and peaceful valleys, but only five acres were cleared. There was a one-room log cabin. It had no window, but light filtered in between the logs where the chinking had fallen out. So did the wind and rain," she laughed.

Courtesy of State Historical Society of Missouri

Household editor for the Ruralist

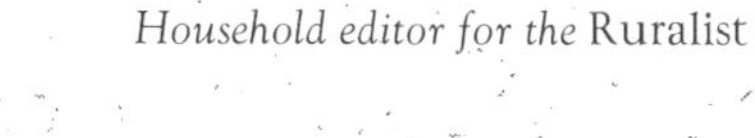

"We dug out a root cellar in the side of a hill and I carried water from the spring.

We built up a herd of dairy cattle and a flock of chickens and cut more trees to add to the house. Almanzo made the furniture.

"My formal education ended with the fifth reader. But soon I was household editor of a farm magazine."

Mrs. Wilder may be alone, but children come from hither and yon to visit, sometimes knocking at 7 in the morning.

Mr. Wilder died in '49 at the age of 92 when they were married 64 years. The only survivor is Mrs. Rose Wilder Lane who lives in Connecticut.

Some of her writings included *Little House on the Prairie, On the Banks of Plum Creek, By the Shores of Silver Lake, The Long Winter, Little Town on the Prairie,* and *Farmer Boy.*

Wilder's Home Just Like Topsy, It Grew As Additional Space Needed

FEATURE ARTICLE IN THE MANSFIELD MIRROR
May 2, 1957

For those citizens of Mansfield who never had the privilege of visiting Mrs. Wilder's home, the Mirror described the house room by room. Visitors to her home today can see many of the treasured items described here. Some of the rooms and furnishings are also mentioned by Neta Seal in chapter five and by the Jones family members in chapter eight. SH

In a home that "just grew" like Topsy, Mrs. Laura Ingalls Wilder spent most of her life in unpretentious surroundings.

Her husband, Almanzo Wilder, didn't need the assistance of an architect to know what they needed for their comfort. As more room was needed, he merely added to the original structure. But it was not as simple as it sounds, for all materials used were found right on the home farm. When lumber was needed, it had to be cut, planed and cured. If stone were needed, he had to cut it. Even the andirons for the fireplace were forged at home by Mr. Wilder.

The setting for the white two-story farm home rests on a hillside about two miles east of Mansfield. The surrounding is considered desirable with a creek, fed by a spring, gurgling along the north side. The shrubbery is primitive and suitable for a home that has been in use for over a half-century. Some of it had been planted by Mr. Wilder, such as the holly which

rambles along the southwest corner. An elm tree flourishes where it was planted within an old tree stump. Across the lawn pecan trees may be seen.

COMFORTABLE ATMOSPHERE

As you enter the front door (but you wouldn't have, for that was not the custom) you would be pleased with the comfortable atmosphere. At the south end of the room was the primitive stone fireplace used to heat the room. On the side wall is an oil painting presented to Mrs. Wilder in 1932. W. M. D. Koerner, artist for the *Saturday Evening Post* at that time, portrayed

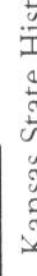

The Wilder home as it looked during the fifties

Mr. and Mrs. Wilder in their youth as they journeyed to Missouri in their covered wagon.

Across the room in the southeast corner was a nook with shelves built up about five feet on four sides which was the library. On the top of the shelves were numerous treasures that were gifts of her daughter, sent from her travels about the world, Mrs. Rose Wilder Lane. But the dearest treasure, no doubt, was the portrait of her daughter when she graduated from high school. But one oil which Mrs. Lane, personally, preferred, was painted by two of her dear friends, Elmer and Berta Hader. These nationally-known illustrators of children's books had given their version of "Telegraph Hill" in San Francisco, California.

COMPANY DINING ROOM

Opposite the library is the "company dining" room, or recess. It contained "Sister Mary's" old walnut organ, dining table, buffet, and a phonograph. The records for the phonograph included Mrs. Wilder's favorite old tunes and records of broadcasts honoring the well-known authoress when she was unable to be present. On the buffet rested a clear glass "Daisy and Button" large size hat, its antiquity an uncertainty, a brass and copper mug with lid, a compote filled with wax fruit, and a pair of lamps.

In the other corner of the room, or to the left of the front entrance, were several windows below which is a window-seat. A cypress table made by Mr. Wilder surrounded by old-fashioned rockers graced this corner, just as in any farm home.

An open stairway went up between the dining room and the window-seat corner. As you stop on the landing a better perspective could be

The stairway with the landing. Mr. Wilder was only 5' 4" and designed the house to fit his size.

gained of the hand-hewn beam cross-wise of the ceiling. The efforts of Mr. Wilder added to instead of detracted from the charm.

HAD HER OWN DEN

Across the landing three steps led downward into a small den, where Mrs. Wilder turned out most of her work. Two sides of the room have windows which give a view of the highway. Though she used a pencil on a common school pad on her lap, her desk showed much use and numerous ink stains.

The rest of the downstairs consists of a bedroom, bath, second dining room (combination of a dining room and living room) and kitchen. All of

Herbert Hoover Presidential Library

The front room with the open stairway in the background

Herbert Hoover Presidential Library

The window-seat corner of the front room

these had the appearance of having been added as they were needed. In the kitchen was an old wood box, for a wood cook-stove was used for heat as well as cooking, as well as a modern range.

If you leave by the "side door" you would be pleased to "tarry awhile" on the huge screened-in porch, with the porch swing swung from the ceiling.

The Story of Rocky Ridge Farm

FEATURE ARTICLE IN THE MISSOURI RURALIST
July 22, 1911

What is successful or not successful sometimes depends on how you look at it. "The Story of Rocky Ridge Farm" was originally published under Almanzo Wilder's name in the Missouri Ruralist *in 1911. However, the piece was no doubt authored by Laura herself as a tribute to her indomitable husband.*

Many men would have given up under the many misfortunes that befell "the Man of the Place," as Laura called him. During their early married years, Almanzo was beset by one disaster after another. A stroke coming after a bout with diphtheria left him paralyzed, and it was only by the exertion of great will that he was able to regain his strength and work his way back to health.

His stroke ended his pioneering in Dakota Territory. He moved his family to Missouri for reasons Laura mentions in the following article. So, at the age of thirty-seven, he started life all over again, taking a rough-hewn Ozark hill farm and turning it into a showplace. SH

To appreciate fully the reason why we named our place Rocky Ridge Farm, it should have been seen at the time of the christening. To begin with it was not bottom land nor by any stretch of the imagination could it have been called second bottom. It was, and is, uncompromisingly ridge land, on the very tip-top of the ridge at that, within a very few miles of the highest point in the Ozarks. And rocky—it certainly was rocky when it was

named, although strangers coming to the place now say, "But why do you call it Rocky Ridge?"

The place looked unpromising enough when we first saw it, not only one but several ridges rolling in every direction and covered with rocks and brush and timber. Perhaps it looked worse to me because I had just left the prairies of South Dakota where the land is easily farmed. I had been ordered south because those prairies had robbed me of my health, and I was glad to

Kansas State Historical Society

Almanzo, center, knew that mules were best for Rocky Ridge travel.

leave them, for they had also robbed me of nearly everything I owned by continual crop failures. Still, coming from such a smooth country, the place looked so rough to me that I hesitated to buy it. But wife had taken a violent fancy to this particular piece of land, saying if she could not have it, she did not want any because it could be made into such a pretty place. It needed the eye of faith, however, to see that in time it could be made very beautiful.

So we bought Rocky Ridge Farm and went to work. We had to put a mortgage on it of $200, and had very little except our bare hands with which to pay it off, improve the farm, and make our living while we did it. It speaks well for the farm, rough and rocky as it was, that my wife and myself with my broken health were able to do all this.

A flock of hens—by the way, there is no better place in the country for raising poultry than right here—a flock of hens and the wood we cleared from the land bought our groceries and clothing. The timber on the place also made rails to fence it and furnished the materials for a large log barn.

At the time I bought it there were on the place four acres cleared and a small log house with a fireplace and no windows. These were practically all the improvements, and there was not grass enough growing on the whole forty acres to keep a cow. The four acres cleared had been set out to apple trees, and enough trees to set twenty acres more were in nursery rows near the house. The land on which to set them was not even cleared of the timber. Luckily, I had bought the place before any serious damage had been done to the fine timber around the building site, although the start had been made to cut it down.

It was hard work and sometimes short rations at the first, but gradually the difficulties were overcome. Land was cleared and prepared by

heroic effort in time to set out all the apple trees, and in a few years the orchard came into bearing. Fields were cleared and brought to a good state of fertility. The timber around the buildings was thinned out enough so that grass would grow between the trees, and each tree would grow in good shape, which has made a beautiful park of the grounds. The rocks have been picked up and grass seed sown so that the pastures and meadows are in fine condition and support quite a little herd of cows, for grass grows remarkably well on "Rocky Ridge" when the timber is cleared away to give it a chance. This good grass and clear spring water make it an ideal dairy farm.

Sixty acres more have been bought and paid for, which, added to the original forty, makes a farm of 100 acres. There is no wasted land on the farm except a wood lot which we have decided to leave permanently for the timber. Perhaps we have not made so much money as farmers in a more level country, but neither have we been obliged to spend so much for expenses; and as the net profit is what counts at the end of the year, I am not afraid to compare the results for a term of years with farms of the same size in a more level country.

Our little Rocky Ridge Farm has supplied everything necessary for a good living and given us good interest on all the money invested every year since the first two. No year has it fallen below ten percent, and one extra good year it paid 100 percent. Besides this, it has doubled in value, and $3,000 more since it was bought.

We are not by any means through with making improvements on Rocky Ridge Farm. There are on the place five springs of running water which never fail even in the driest season. Some of these springs are so situated that by building a dam below them, a lake of three acres, twenty feet deep in places, will be near the house. Another small lake can be made in the same way in the duck pasture, and these are planned for the near future.

But the first thing on the improvement program is building a cement tank as a reservoir around a spring which is higher than the buildings. Water from this tank will be piped down and supply water in the house and barn and in the poultry yards.

When I look around the farm now and see the smooth, green, rolling meadows and pastures, the good fields of corn and wheat and oats, when I see the orchard and strawberry field like huge bouquets in the spring or full of fruit later in the season, when I see the grapevines hanging full of luscious grapes, I can hardly bring back to my mind the rough, rocky, brushy, ugly place that we first called Rocky Ridge Farm. The name given it then serves to remind us of the battles we have fought and won and gives a touch of sentiment and an added value to the place.

In conclusion, I am going to quote from a little gift book which my wife sent out to a few friends last Christmas:

> Just come and visit Rocky Ridge,
> Please grant us our request;
> We'll give you all a jolly time—
> Welcome the coming; speed the parting guest.

My Apple Orchard

FEATURE ARTICLE IN THE MISSOURI RURALIST
June 1, 1912

Laura Ingalls Wilder loved to tell of her husband's accomplishments and followed "The Story of Rocky Ridge Farm" with an article about their most effective early enterprise: the farm's apple orchard.

Writing again as Almanzo, Laura describes activities that could have been written for the organically correct Mother Earth News. *Quail kill tree worms rather than chemicals; no hunting is permitted on the farm. Hard work rather than technology gets the job done. And that orchard did produce a solid income for many years, the first visible sign that the Wilders might be turning the corner in their fight with poverty.*

Alas, the orchard is no more! Time and an unpredictable market for fruit led the Wilders in other directions. Poultry and dairy farming became their mainstays. But the planting and nurturing of their apple orchard permitted Laura and Almanzo the opportunity to boast after years of economic humiliation. Rose never quite got over the horror and embarrassment of her parents' struggle, but she thought them remarkable for the way they endured it. SH

When I bought my farm in the fall, some years ago, there were 800 apple trees on it growing in nursery rows. Two hundred had been set out the spring before, in an old worn-out field, where the land was so poor it would not raise a stalk of corn over four feet high. This field was all the land cleared on the place; the rest of the farm was covered with oak timber.

MISSOURI RURALIST

WITH WHICH IS COMBINED THE BREEDERS SPECIAL

A WEEKLY JOURNAL FOR MISSOURI FARMERS AND BREEDERS

Vol. IX, Whole No. 503 | Saturday, June 1, 1912 | Price $1.00 Per Year

FROM this 12 year old apple tree in the Ozark country of Missouri were gathered at one time five barrels [illegible] No. 1, and three barrels of No. 2 apples. They were highly colored and of most excellent flavor. This tree is a sam[illegible] of the trees on the hundred-acre orchard farm of A. J. Wilder, who is shown standing at the side of the tree. Aft[illegible]ruitless struggle on the plains of Dakota, Mr. Wilder came to Missouri, settling at Mansfield. He purchased 40 acres o[illegible]eveloped land by going in debt for it and went to work. Mother Nature rewarded his well meant if not well direc[illegible]forts—he knew nothing of orcharding at the time. Mr. Wilder has since added another 60 acres. He is out of debt, [illegible] has more than doubled in value and his orchard is regarded by nurserymen and apple buyers as one of the bes[illegible] Ozark country.

Kansas State Historical Society

"The Man of the Place" by one of his many fine apple trees

I have always thought it must have been a good agent who persuaded the man of whom I bought the place to mortgage it for 1,000 apple trees when the ground was not even cleared on which to set them. However, he unloaded his blunder onto me, and I knew nothing about an orchard, did not even know one apple from another. I did know though that apple trees, or indeed trees of any kind, could not be expected to thrive in land too poor to raise corn fodder, so whenever I made a trip to town, I brought back a load of wood ashes from the mill or a load of manure from the livery barn and put it around those trees that were already set out in the field.

I cleared enough land that winter on which to set out the trees from the nursery, broke it the next spring, and put in the trees after I had worked it as smooth as I could. The trees already set out were 25 feet apart in the rows and 32 feet between the rows, so I set the others the same way. I dug the holes for the trees large and deep, making the dirt fine in the bottom and mixing some wood ashes with it.

I handled the trees very carefully so as not to injure the roots and spread the roots out as nearly as possible in a natural manner when setting the trees. Fine dirt was put over the roots at first and pressed down firmly, then the dirt was shoveled in to fill the hole. Some more wood ashes were mixed with the dirt when it was being shoveled in. I did not hill the dirt up around the tree but left it a little cupping for conserving moisture. All trash was raked away, leaving it clean and smooth, and again I used some wood ashes, scattering them around the tree, but being careful that none touched it to injure the bark. The ashes were used altogether with the idea of fertilizing the soil and with no idea of any other benefit, but I think they may have saved my orchard.

It is confessing to a colossal ignorance, but I found out later that I planted wooly aphis [aphids] on nearly every one of my apple tree roots. At

the time, I thought that for some reason they were a little moldy. I read afterward in an orchard paper that the lye from wood ashes would destroy the wooly aphis and save the tree; and as the use of wood ashes around the trees was kept up for several years, I give them the credit for saving my trees.

As I never allowed hunting on the farm, the quail were thick in the orchard and used to wallow and dust themselves like chickens in this fine dirt close to the tree. I wish this fact to be particularly noted in connection with the other fact that I had no borers in my trees for years.

A near neighbor set out 2,000 trees about the same time and lost seven-eighths of them because of borers. He used every possible means to rid his trees of them except the simple one of letting the quail and other birds live in his orchard. Instead, he allowed his boys to kill every bird they saw.

My apples were sound and smooth, not wormy, which I also credit to the birds for catching insects of all kinds as I never sprayed the trees. Within the last few years, the hunters, both boys and men, have been so active that it has been impossible to save my quail; and so I have had to begin the eternal round of spraying and cutting the trees to get the borers out.

When I set the trees I trimmed them back a good deal. While I knew nothing of the science of trimming I knew that I did not want a forked tree, so I trimmed to one stem with a few little branches left at the top. I watched the trees as they grew and trimmed away, while they were very small, all the branches that would interlock or rub against another branch.

In the fall I always whitewashed the trees to keep the rabbits from gnawing the bark, and if the storms washed it off, I whitewashed them again. Every spring they were whitewashed in April as a sort of house-cleaning and to make the bark smooth so it would not harbor insects, for I found that if there was a rough place, that was where the eggs of insects were deposited.

Between the trees, I raised corn, potatoes, and garden until the trees

were eight years old when I seeded that land down to timothy and clover. Of course, when I raised crops, I fertilized them enough to make them grow, and the trees always got their share. As a result, I get a good hay crop out of the orchard, making two good crops from the land.

I think that one thing that has made my orchard a success is that I took individual care of each tree. What that particular tree needed it got. Wife and I were so well acquainted with the trees that if I wished to mention one to her, I would say "that tree with the large branch to the south," or "the tree that leans to the north," etc. The tree that leaned was gently taught to stand straight so that the sun would not burn the bark. This was done by tying it to a stake firmly driven into the ground on the south side of the tree and from time to time shortening the string which held it.

The trees came into bearing at seven years old, and the apples were extra well colored and smooth skinned. I have had apple buyers and nurserymen tell me that my orchard was the prettiest they ever saw, and my Ben Davis are different from any I have ever seen in being better colored and flavored and in the texture of the flesh. People even refuse to believe that they are Ben Davis at times. My orchard is mostly Ben Davis, and the rest is Missouri Pippin.

If I were to start another orchard, I would plow and cultivate the land for several seasons to prepare it for the trees. The wildness and roughness should be worked out in order to give the little trees a fair chance. Then I should plant apple seed where I wanted the trees to stand, and then bud onto the sprout the variety I wished to raise. In this way the taproot would not be disturbed, as it is by moving the tree, but would run straight down. This makes a longer-lived, stronger tree.

The Life of Laura Ingalls Wilder

FEATURE ARTICLE IN THE MANSFIELD MIRROR
September 18, 1986

Every year Mansfield puts on a festival where there will be plenty of good things to eat, crafts on display, and a special article in the Mansfield Mirror *recounting the story of Mrs. Wilder's life. You will always be welcome at a Laura Ingalls Wilder Day celebration.*

This September 1986 article gives a good overview of Mrs. Wilder's story up to the time she began writing her famous children's books. As always there is a question about dates. A particular event will be mentioned as happening a certain year in one article and then will be placed in another year in a different source.

The truth is, the dates are usually only one or two years off. Such slight discrepancies are amazing considering that the busy Mrs. Wilder did not keep a diary. Only recently, it has been discovered that the Wilders were able to purchase a small house in De Smet, only two years prior to their giving up life in De Smet entirely. So the move to Mansfield in 1894 may have been more of a spur-of-the-moment decision than anyone has heretofore thought! SH

On February 7, 1867, a little girl was born to Charles and Caroline Ingalls. The baby was christened Laura Elizabeth. She was the second daughter of four to be born to the Ingallses.

The daughter to precede Laura in birth was Mary Amelia (January 10, 1865). With these two daughters and wife, Charles Ingalls farmed a small farm in Wisconsin that was later to be known as "Little House in the Big Woods."

But Pa Ingalls was a pioneer and could not stand to stay in one place for long at one time, so he bundled up his three ladies and put them into a covered wagon and headed for Montgomery County, Kansas. Here in the family's second log cabin, Charles started farming anew.

A wonderful event came to grace the Ingalls again when their third daughter Carrie was born on August 3, 1870. But their life there was to be short-lived, for the government decided that the settlers were on Indian land and must either move out or be moved out by federal troops. Charles packed up his family once again and moved on to Minnesota.

In Plum Creek, Minnesota, the family seemed at last to have found a home where they could stay and prosper. There was a school for the girls to attend and a church to join, and it appeared to be Jordan across from Caanan. Even a son, Charles Frederick, was born to the Ingallses on November 1, 1875 [he died in 1876]. But the good times were not to continue, for grasshoppers ruined the Ingallses' crops and work was then very hard to find for Pa Ingalls. He was forced to travel far and wide to find the funds to feed his growing family.

So it was decided to move again. The family of six now (Grace Pearl, May 23, 1871 [1877]) headed for Burr Oak, Iowa. They stayed for only a short time and then returned to Minnesota.

Trouble plagued the family in 1879 when all the girls except Laura came down with scarlet fever. All survived, but Mary lost her sight for the rest of her life. The house was saddened by this unfortunate event, but a situation presented itself to Pa to take a job in De Smet in the Dakota Territory.

Pa worked for the railroad there and the family was very happy. Pa was able to homestead a claim and the girls were able to go to school and the family attended a church that they helped found, the De Smet First

Congregational Church. Things were working out so well that even Mary, though blind, could still go to college.

Happiness was also in store for 18-year-old Laura. In 1885 she married Almanzo Wilder. Almanzo had a claim on some land near De Smet, and Laura helped him work it. In 1886 Almanzo and Laura Wilder presented their parents with a granddaughter named Rose.

Everything looked prosperous and full of happiness and fullness of life for the Wilders in the Dakota Territory, but it was not to be. All of the crops were destroyed year after year by either hail or wind or drought or grasshoppers. Diphtheria struck the young family and almost destroyed Almanzo's health.

Fire took their home completely in 1889 and then came five years of drought from 1881–1885. They held on in the Dakota Territory until 1890 when they moved to Spring Lake, Minnesota. [Dates *sic.*]

After only a short time they decided that for Almanzo's sake they had better move to a better climate, so off they went to Florida. Florida did not suit the Wilders and as Laura was to say to Irene Lichty, curator of the Wilder Home and Museum, many years later, "I will never go back to Florida as it is too low for me there."

By the middle of the year 1892, the family of three was back in De Smet where Almanzo did odd jobs to support his family. Laura assisted in the family finances by becoming a seamstress for a dollar a day. Rose now age five, was allowed to attend school because her mother and father worked all day.

Laura Ingalls Wilder, though, had an ingrained sense of the pioneer. She had been raised all of her life as a pioneer girl, and even when she married, she happened to pick another pioneer who loved to roam our beautiful country. Almanzo decided that it was time to leave on yet another

journey, and so, on July 17, 1894, the little family of three left for the Ozarks of Missouri.

The Wilders entered the state of Missouri on August 22, 1894. They arrived at what was to be their final home, Mansfield, after traveling 650 miles in 45 days. The Ozarks with its fall foliage in great array was no doubt a beautiful sight to three weary travelers who had been used to a dusty, windy, and hot climate like De Smet.

With the hundred hard earned dollars that Laura had saved from her long hours as a seamstress, she and Almanzo decided to buy a forty-acre plot of rocky, hilly land that was located one mile to the east of Mansfield. The hundred dollars went for the down payment. The entire plot of forty acres consisted of only five acres of cleared land, 400 unplanted apple trees, and a one-room windowless log cabin. Laura named their ground Rocky Ridge Farm.

The hard work of turning Rocky Ridge into a farm was just beginning and would take the Wilders many years to complete. Their neighbors pitched in as all pioneer neighbors did and helped Almanzo, Laura, and Rose build a hen house and a stable. Their first crop of corn was planted in 1895 along with potatoes. With egg and potato money, and money earned from the sale of wood and berries picked by Rose, the Wilders were finally able to purchase a pig and a cow.

A short time after their final home was started, the Wilders moved into Mansfield to make more money by taking in boarders and feeding the railroad workers that then resided in Mansfield. The house in which they lived in Mansfield was presented to the Wilders as a gift by Almanzo's father when he and his family came to visit in 1897. Just a few years later the Wilders decided that the farm was the place for them and they sold the Mansfield house and moved back to the farm just outside of Mansfield.

It was now decided that Rose would have to go elsewhere for her schooling for she had about run to the limit of the amount of learning that could be obtained in Mansfield. Almanzo and Laura sent Rose to Louisiana to attend high school and live with Almanzo's sister, Eliza Jane. Rose was a good student, as always, and graduated in 1903.

Back at home at Rocky Ridge things were going very well. The farm in time would be up to 200 acres and the fruit from the farm would be making it all the way to markets in the big cities. Almanzo even brought in the Magnificent Morgan breed of horses to increase the quality of his own horses and that of his neighbors. Even the home was continuing to grow in size taking better shape year by year. Almanzo spared no labor on the home that was going to be for his beloved Laura.

Laura's kitchen was considered to be, at one time, the most modern in the Ozarks. The home was finally completed in 1912 and was indeed an Ozark showplace.

Laura's kitchen was considered . . . the most modern in the Ozarks.

More vistas that were not even dreamed about were to open for the now very content Almanzo and Laura. Laura had been making speeches concerning the raising of poultry which she did so well, and as she was unable to attend one of the meetings, she wrote out her speech so that it could be read. An editor of the *Missouri Ruralist* was in the audience and he offered Laura the job as home editor. She accepted.

In February of 1911 Laura Ingalls Wilder was a writer! Her writings about the raising of poultry and other farm tasks gradually gained access to many other newspapers and magazines. This added occupation also allowed Laura little extras for the home that she would not have otherwise had and also allowed her to travel to see her mother and sisters in De Smet. She even traveled to the west coast to visit Rose and her husband.

Back in Mansfield Laura and Almanzo continued to work hard and prosper. Laura loved to work and to this end she took it upon herself to start a library at the county seat in Hartville and neighboring towns. She also became a member of many clubs and organizations, helping them to prosper with her hard work and dogged determination. Laura worked also with many women's farm clubs. Along this line, she worked with the Mansfield Farm Loan Association. She handed out almost a million dollars and not once was the money not repaid.

Rose Wilder Lane, Almanzo and Laura's daughter, was now becoming famous in her own right. Rose had been sent as a reporter to cover the war overseas. From her comments and articles the Wilders could follow her progress through many foreign lands. Rose was also writing books, two of which were *Henry Ford's Own Story* and *Peaks of Shala*. Rose came home to Rocky Ridge Farm after the war a wealthy person. She had a home built on the family land not far from the main house and lived there for several years.

Retirement was coming for the Wilders and when the new Highway 60 came through Rocky Ridge, the Wilders started selling off the land that had been their livelihood for 35 years. Many years Almanzo and Laura had worked for the day when they could sit back and rest and enjoy their well-deserved retirement.

The 1930s rolled in and Rose requested that Laura write down some of the old family stories so that they would not be lost. Laura complied and sent them to Rose thinking that Rose would write them into a book. Rose returned them to Laura and said, you write the book! So in 1932 at the age of 65, "retired" Laura Ingalls Wilder sent a book to Harper and Brothers entitled *Little House in the Big Woods*. A new career was just starting.

Mansfield Woman's Books Favored Both by Children and Grown-ups World Acclaim Has Come to Laura Ingalls Wilder Whose Writings Cover Pioneer Life

FEATURE ARTICLE IN THE MANSFIELD MIRROR
May 5, 1949

The following feature story by Chester Bradley of the Kansas City Star *appeared in that paper on Sunday, April 10, 1949 and is used by permission. The* Mirror *reprinted it in May. I find it of special value because it touches on Mrs. Wilder's feelings about income taxes, which for most of her life she had never had to deal with. There were even years, when she and Almanzo were approaching prosperity, where they deliberately limited their income, much as we find tax lawyers advising us to do today!*

Mrs. Wilder was politically what would be known as an early Progressive, but she never found taxes on those who had labored their way to prosperity to be an incentive for even more labor.

Surely the years from the end of World War II to her husband's death in 1949 were the happy golden years of Laura's life. Her habit of frugality remained, but the necessity for it was gone. It was in a somewhat reflective vein, then, that she gave this interview to Chester Bradley. SH

Mansfield, Mo., April 9—Stories of Middle Western American pioneer life which were written here on a school tablet with a pencil are being read

around the world and by millions of Americans. Their author, Laura Ingalls Wilder, 82, is known and loved by countless school children. Their parents also like her "Laura and Mary" stories.

By all standards Mrs. Wilder is a famous American author. Nevertheless, she is unaffected and as unassuming as in her earlier days when she helped "pull a crosscut saw" on Ozark timber.

This month the city of Detroit is paying high tribute to Mrs. Wilder. It is naming one of its new branch libraries for her. Other such libraries there bear some of the most famous names in American history.

Mrs. Wilder is the author of eight books that tell a story of everyday life in early Western America, extending from Wisconsin to the Dakotas and including adventures into the Indian territory of Kansas. Seven of the volumes are "Laura and Mary" stories, these characters being representative of Mrs. Wilder and a sister named Mary. The other book in the series is the story of a year in the boyhood life of her husband, Almanzo Wilder, who is 92 and a native of New York.

Live in Distinctive Home

This Ozark town of a little more than 1,000 population is 250 miles southwest of Kansas City. [Editor's note: This misstatement couldn't go by; 250 miles southwest of Kansas City will put you in Oklahoma!] The Wilders live a half mile east of it. Their unpretentious, 2-story, white frame house sits on a hill overlooking U.S. highway No. 60. It has a vine-covered, stone chimney, tall and wide. Inside the home it is connected with a large fireplace in the living room—a room at once distinctive to a visitor because of its beamed ceiling and liberal use of woodwork, all white oak cut on the farm and shaped into lumber by the Wilders years ago. Except for the

siding, most all materials used in building the home came right off the farm.

The living room also has several wall cases and shelves for the many books of the family library and there are framed scrolls and other pieces of art, written or painted in tribute to Mrs. Wilder's stories.

Mr. and Mrs. Wilder have lived in this home on the land they call Rocky Ridge Farm since they moved here in a covered wagon from De Smet, S. D., in 1894. A drought lasting nearly three years had ruined most everything and everybody in the Dakotas, so the Wilders set out for the Ozarks, then known as "the land of the big red apples," seeking a new start in life.

They lived here in town for awhile, then acquired forty acres nearby, including a tree lien on the place. That proviso of the deal required that they carry out the terms of a former owner—to plant apple trees. The Wilders did, some ten acres at first, and their orchards were tended well enough that production reached proportions of carload shipments to Memphis, Tennessee, and other markets. Mrs. Wilder recalls that spraying was virtually unknown and unneeded in those days.

By the hardest of work in their earlier years here—Mrs. Wilder remembering well having helped to pull a saw on timber—they expanded their farm to more than 200 acres, had many chickens and dairy cattle and kept farm work going until recent years.

"We worked hard, but it was interesting and didn't hurt us any," Mrs. Wilder says.

SHE RAISED CHICKENS

Their farm was made one of the most successful hereabouts. Mrs. Wilder raised the chickens and her husband handled the cows. Once they

had a contest, she says, as to whether cows or chickens brought the biggest returns.

"We had to work against each other trying to prove our point," she adds with a brightening of the eyes, adding quickly that the contest "ended in a draw."

The Wilders take pride in their long years of work and in the success they made on their Ozark farmland. Mrs. Wilder is much less willing to talk of her success as a writer or of any claim to fame. She disdains having any display made over her writing, although it has attained a place that brings fan mail from Japan, Sweden, and other countries as well as points all around America.

Her first writings were for newspapers and magazines, usually on poultry, or farming and rural subjects. It was not until 1932 that her first book was published and this event was more or less unexpected as far as she was concerned.

"Pa" Ingalls, her father, was a pioneer hunter, trapper, and Indian fighter. He guarded property of the Chicago-Northwestern railroad in the days it was being built, had many adventures in the Middle West and became one of the founders of De Smet, S. D.

Time after time she had heard him tell of his experiences and her own part in the family activities are worth reading, as proven by book sales today.

"These were family stories and I believed they should be preserved," Mrs. Wilder said, "so I wrote some of them down and sent them to my daughter Rose, so she could keep them. I also suggested she might want to use some of them in her writings."

Rose Wilder Lane, her daughter, who lives in Danbury, Conn., already was nationally known as a reporter and author.

"Rose wrote back, some time later," Mrs. Wilder continued, "that an editor had said the stories could be published if I would put some meat on the bones; so after that I started doing just that.

"I wrote between washing dishes and getting dinner, or just any time I could," she added. "But sometimes I got stumped on a phrase or a chapter. Maybe the way to do it would not come to me until after I had gone to bed and then I would think of something in the middle of the night."

Thus the many duties of an active farm wife took on new chores, but highly worthwhile ones.

She used an ordinary pencil and school tablet. Her manuscripts were sent to New York for typing, and all business connected with the work of publication was and is handled by her agent. He is George T. Bye, former Kansas Citian, who handles the writing of Mrs. Franklin D. (Eleanor) Roosevelt, and other celebrities.

FAVORITE AMONG CHILDREN

Harper & Brothers of New York published the first book by Mrs. Wilder and all the others in the series. Chicago school children in 1947 selected Mrs. Wilder as their favorite author. She was honored in a special radio broadcast there. A plaque in the home here contains signatures of many Chicago children who took part in the events. Similar plaques have come from the Association of Children's Librarians of Northern California; also one from Seattle, representing children and librarians of the Pacific Northwest.

Her books are very popular with Kansas City Public Library patrons. "Pa's Fiddle," well known in the books now is in the state museum at Pierre, S. D., but is played every year in a special annual concert there.

With fame and extra cash from book royalties in recent years, most persons would say the golden years are certainly continuing, but writing success has its drawbacks these days, Mrs. Wilder finds.

HIT BY INCOME TAX

"The more I wrote the bigger my income tax got, so I stopped."

She doesn't talk in figures of the money she has received for her books, but she says: "The more I wrote the bigger my income tax got, so I stopped. Why should I go on at my age? Why, we don't need it here anyway."

The latter statement was in regard to her complete satisfaction with the simple, comfortable life in the home she has known for more than half a century, their home until the end of their days. But they still have a garden.

"I just finished planting the potatoes," said Mr. Wilder as he entered the home to greet visitors. Despite "not being strong" and his 92 years, he is most alert to the current scene. Both the Wilders, however, complain of not being able to get help, "either inside or outside the house."

Detroit is planning appropriate ceremonies for the dedication of the library named for Mrs. Wilder. Officials there are eager for Mrs. Wilder to take part, but she says "definitely" she will not. It would be too much of a trip for Mr. Wilder, she adds; also, while she feels well, and certainly looks it, she says, "I'm too nervous" for anything like that.

Her last public appearance as an author was in Detroit six years ago when she took part in book week events there.

Ralph A. Ulveling, library director of Detroit, said recently that "we believe her books will live and will be read with interest a hundred years from now just as they are today. If our prediction is correct we will naturally take particular pride in having been the institution that led the way in bringing her permanent recognition among the American men and women of letters."

Others honored similarly by Detroit libraries include such famous Americans as Thomas Jefferson, Abraham Lincoln, and Thomas A. Edison, Ulveling noted. Seldom has the city so honored any living person.

"In choosing the name of Mrs. Wilder," Ulveling said, "we did so because we felt that she was a Midwestern writer who in her series of books has presented an invaluable social history of this great central portion of the country. While some historians, and they have an important place, present the great sweep of history, bringing out the political and the military influences, Mrs. Wilder has directed attention to the commonplace things, the way of life of people. Thus she has preserved a portion of our history which is the part that is most likely to be lost in the course of time. She has done this beautifully, ably, and understandably, and like so few writers she has done it in a way which is interesting both to children and to adults."

CHAPTER 5

Friends and Travelers: The Personal Recollections of Neta Seal

I may surprise you when I assert this, but I remember Laura Ingalls Wilder myself—in a way. Although she died when I was only eight, I remember Laura through her own writings, through Neva Whaley Harding's reminiscence, through the records of the little towns of De Smet and Mansfield.

But I also remember Laura—"the pint of cider half drunk up," as Pa Ingalls used to call her—in a more intimate fashion through the eyes of her friends and neighbors with whom I have personally spoken.

It is hard to explain the thrill of it, but Laura is no longer long ago and far away when I meet Sheldon and Iola Jones, who lived on the farm next to her, or when I talk to Neta Seal and Nava Austin, who were close friends. In their voices and in their anecdotes, the past comes alive—no, I take that back, the past isn't even past anymore.

Neta Seal may be the genuine evidence that "they really don't make them like they used to." Devoted partner with her husband, Silas, she helped him build up his garage business in the small town of Mansfield, Missouri; owned rental property, which she continued to manage after his death; and took in washing for a time.

But Mrs. Seal was never too busy to be with people, and she was, at eighty-nine, just after a serious operation, still a people-person. One of the persons she grew attached to was Mrs. A. J. Wilder—Laura Ingalls Wilder.

Mrs. Seal first met Laura in the late 1930s, and their friendship grew fast and strong throughout the remaining twenty years of Laura's life. Fortunately for us, Neta Seal has the remarkable attribute of a fine memory, and she has shared her knowledge of Mr. and Mrs. Wilder with hundreds of people over the years. SH

Mrs. Seal dressed in clothes that once belonged to Laura

"Seal, you don't know whether I'm going to buy a dime's worth of gas from you."

How we met the Wilders is sort of a long story. We came back from Detroit and bought a filling station, or a service station, we called it then, because it was all service.

One morning Almanzo came in and my husband checked his tires and cleaned his windshield and his windows and said, with a smile, "Mr. Wilder, what will you have?"

"Seal, you don't know whether I'm going to buy a dime's worth of gas from you," Mr. Wilder said, "but you give me all this free service, then ask me what I want."

"Well, Mr. Wilder you need your windshield cleaned, and you need the right amount of air in your tires if you are going to drive," my husband replied. And that made a friend.

Mr. Wilder was always in there after that. He'd come into the service station and let Mrs. Wilder out—he called her Bessie and she called him Manly—to go to the grocery store, to the bank, or whatever she wanted to do. It was the kind of place where people gathered to talk. We sold gas and oil and all those things, and folks would just come down. I would say that Mrs. Wilder was the more outgoing and had a pretty good sense of humor.

By the time we got acquainted with them both, Mr. Wilder was

crippled and used a cane. He walked with a limp and had one club foot. His shoe had to have a real thick sole, but I don't remember which foot it was. I think it was his right one, but I'm not sure.

Almanzo didn't have horses anymore; he had sold them. But he did have some goats. I can't remember exactly how many he had, maybe four or five, maybe six. He didn't have a big herd of them. These were milk goats, and he milked them by hand. He had a barn, and he had a little stand for them to step up on, and he'd go out there, and they'd come and jump up on it. He'd sit down and milk one; then he would turn that one out and let the next one in. But finally he got to where he couldn't take care of them so he sold them.

He called her Bessie and she called him Manly.

They always had a dog up till old Ben died. He was a bulldog. They always had bulldogs after I got acquainted with them—I never knew them to have a cat.

Here's a funny little story about the dog. He had a boil on his jaw; and when it went to hurting him so bad, he'd come in and lay his head in her lap and look up as if he was saying, "Can you do anything for me?" Then she would get some salve and rub it on his jaw. When that was done, he would go back and lay down. Finally, it was healed.

Mrs. Wilder—I always called her Mrs. Wilder—didn't even have a dog after he went away [Almanzo died in 1949].

GOING WEST WITH THE WILDERS

You know, I did meet some of her family. We had come back from Detroit and had bought the filling station, but they were going to have to work on the streets, pave them or something. We didn't have anything to do, but Mr. Wilder wanted my husband to drive them on a trip to California [in 1938].

So my husband came in one day and asked me if I would like a trip to California with the Wilders. I hesitated a minute, then replied: "I don't know them well enough to make a long trip with them."

"Now is a good time to become acquainted. All it will cost us is money for our meals and lodging." You could get cabins for fifty cents a night then.

We left Mansfield early in May and got back by the end of the month.

SINGING WITH MRS. WILDER

On the trip we sang little crazy songs, Mrs. Wilder and I did, in the back seat, just to pass the time away:

> Waltz me around, O Willy,
> Around and around and around.
> And I'll give you some kisses
> To make up for misses,
> So waltz me around and around.

She loved that one because it was kind of fast. We'd just sing it over and over. Another one was "She Drives a Cadillac":

> She drives a Cadillac;
> I walk to work and back.
> Oh boy, that's where my money goes.
> My money goes

To buy my baby clothes.
(I buy her everything
for to keep her in style.)

She drives a little red Ford;
I ride the running board.
Oh boy, that's where my money goes.

While on our journey, Mr. Wilder was collecting branches to make walking canes. He really wanted a cane from each state in the Union. During a stop, he saw a tree he wanted a branch from for a cane. My husband cut the branch from the tree, and as they drove away, they came upon this sign: "This Park Protected by Law." They were certainly happy they hadn't been caught.

Mrs. Wilder tried to find a native Californian, but it seemed that everyone she talked to were natives of other states. One day we were sightseeing when Mrs. Wilder called excitedly, "I've found a native!" The man knew their daughter, Rose Wilder Lane, so they had a delightful visit with him.

Yes, it was quite a trip because we came back by way of the Black Hills of South Dakota. Laura's sister Carrie was living there in Keystone right by Mt. Rushmore. So we got us a cabin, and they stayed with Carrie.

She was about the same size as Laura, small, and she was really nice. A year or two after this visit, Carrie came down to Mansfield to visit, and we were with them quite a while because we would take them driving to see different parts of the Ozarks.

Carrie's husband wasn't with her; he had died.

Laura's sister Grace was also still living over at De Smet. Grace was taller than either Laura or Carrie, as I remember. She was built more like Rose, but she was a little plump, not fat. I don't remember Grace visiting the Wilders in Mansfield while I knew them.

When we took that trip, I think Mrs. Wilder had finished her books. Maybe not all of them. But she had done most of the writing. I got autographed copies of all of them. She gave me the full set with the statement: "You're not to loan these to anybody. If they want to read them they can go to the library or buy them. Because if you start loaning them out they'll be torn up, and they'll be lost and you won't have them." So I've never loaned them.

We weren't members of any of the same clubs, but after that trip we were fast friends. I was a Baptist and she was a Methodist, and I didn't attend a lot of clubs. They were both pretty much retired when we knew them. And they did have a modern farmhouse. Water was piped up to the house from a little ravine in back that had a spring. They also had indoor plumbing and a bathroom, though they didn't use modern heat. It was propane. We don't have natural gas down here even now.

MR. WILDER

In his retirement, Mr. Wilder had a shop that kept him busy. He'd go putter in that shop. Now we built an apartment house, and we lived in part of it and rented the other part—just two rooms—and Mr. Wilder got it in his head that he wanted to move into one of them apartments.

Mrs. Wilder told me, "He just pesters me to death to move into one of them apartments." So she said, "One day I told him, I said, 'Now, Manly, you

go out to your workshop; we can't take that with us, you know. You'll have to sort it out and sell it. Now you go out there and make a list of anything you're going to sell before we move in.' "

He went out there and was gone quite a while. When he came back, he never said another word about moving from that time until he died. He didn't want to get rid of his workshop.

Mr. Wilder could make beautiful furniture. He once gave us a table that was made out of a cypress tree he brought back from Florida. It's back in their old home now. We let the home have it because it would mean a lot to the public to see that. And then he gave us a big, wide-armed chair he made out of sassafras. We left that in the home too, just like it was when they lived there.

I don't know whatever happened to the apple orchard [Almanzo had a large orchard at one time]. It's all gone. I imagine it just rotted. After we got to know them, they sold the biggest part of their farm to the Shorters. It was just too much for him to look after. They made payments to Mr. Wilder rather than pay full price because he said, "I want some income. I'll let him pay it out in payments each month and then I'll have some money."

THE FINAL YEARS

As I remember, Mrs. Wilder remained pretty healthy for a time even after Almanzo died. She did some sewing, crocheting and embroidery, but not too much.

After he passed away, we went out there every Sunday afternoon to see her. We'd take her for drives. For a while she owned a Chrysler, I think, then she sold it.

There was a man by the name of Mr. Hartley here in town who was a

taxi driver. So she finally let him go get her and bring her to town for the groceries. I had always done that and taken her to the bank, but I had this apartment house with four sleeping rooms I rented by night. It got to be too much work, so she let him drive her. Helen Burkhiser did a book on me [*Neta, Laura's Friend*, available through the home and museum in Mansfield, Missouri] that exhausted me when I saw what all I had done.

Mrs. Wilder passed her time by doing a lot of reading, I think. That was until her eyes failed. She did like to keep the radio on, but I don't remember what she listened to. I don't remember there ever being any TV.

I don't remember as good as I used to. For example, I don't remember any of her favorite foods except that both her and Almanzo especially liked my Swiss steak. And I don't remember her saying that she had a favorite of her own books, but she did talk about her family, the whole family, but more about her sisters Mary and Grace.

Oh, Mrs. Wilder did get letters from school children, letters and letters and letters. At first, she answered each one individually, but then her eyes began to fail her. She had diabetes, and that's what caused it. Anyway, she got to where she'd just write the teacher a letter and let her read it to all the children. She even got letters from Japan.

Since then many Japanese have come to Mansfield to visit the home. One summer [1991] they even made a movie of this place, took a helicopter and flew it all over the little town of Mansfield. They took pictures at the farm and at the school.

Mrs. Wilder and her daughter, Rose, stayed in close touch, both by telephone and by letter. I don't think Rose made it to her father's funeral. She did come down before her mother's final illness, while Mrs. Wilder was in the Springfield hospital.

One of the things we did while she was in the hospital was to take

Mrs. Wilder water out of her own well. We would take her jugs of water every time we went to see her. She didn't like the Springfield water.

Mrs. Wilder was able to come home from the hospital to the house she and Mr. Wilder had built together. Not much later she died there in the home.

CHAPTER 6

Weekly Visits with Laura: The Personal Recollections of Nava Austin

Nava Austin is the head librarian for the Wright County, Missouri, libraries. She presides over several institutions, small though they may be, that are widely scattered. To talk to Nava Austin, you have to talk on the run.

Ms. Austin has been a librarian for the county some forty years and was present when the Mansfield library was named in honor of Laura Ingalls Wilder in September of 1951. She probably knows the history of Wright County as well as anyone.

Mrs. Wilder loved the library and loved to visit with Ms. Austin when she came to town. Mrs. Wilder's will made provision for the library, and it eventually received over $25,000 on the royalty proceeds of two of Wilder's books.

Stop by the library if you ever visit Mrs. Wilder's home. The library has a collection of dolls given to Mrs. Wilder that accurately depict her famous pioneering family in period costume. There are also additional photographs of Laura there. SH

I knew Mrs. Wilder from 1951 to 1955. In 1955 her health failed, and she wasn't able to come in, as she had, every Wednesday morning for those years.

When I first got to know her, I was assistant librarian at Mansfield. She did come in every Wednesday morning to town and to the library.

There was an elderly lady in town whose name I forget—she must have been around ninety—that Mrs. Wilder would go down and have tea with. But she always said coming to the library was the highlight of her day.

Later on, she would eat lunch, most of the time at the Owens Cafe.

Used by permission of Larry Dennis

Laura, center, at the library named in her honor

Then Mr. Hartley would drive her down to the town of Ava because she enjoyed the scenery and the outdoors.

One day, Mrs. Wilder came into the library and said, "I want you to have lunch with me. I got a surprise in the mail this morning."

"What was that?" I asked.

"Well, I got a $500 royalty check that I wasn't expecting!"

Although we didn't usually close over lunch hour, she said, "I'll go on up to the cafe and order us a shrimp dinner, and then you can come up to the cafe and take time to eat a shrimp dinner with me." So I did.

One day Mrs. Wilder came to the library and made a tape for me on old reel-to-reel recorders. I taped her conversation, and I taped the questions, some of which had come from children in letters they had written to her.

The sort of questions we asked her on the tape had to do with how old she was when she first began her books [sixty-five]. Would you care to describe each doll a little bit? Did Mary wear her bonnet better than you did and was her hair lighter than yours? [The answer to both questions was yes.] Would you care to tell what happened to Mary? [After Mary finished college, she lived with Ma for the rest of her life.]

We do have her doll collection, made by a Barbara Brooks in California, here at the library. They're kind of interesting. The dolls are little character dolls and show Ma sitting in her rocking chair holding baby Grace. Pa has his fiddle, and Almanzo is shown as a farmer boy who loved to fish. Mrs. Wilder felt that they were accurately made; for example, Pa had a reddish beard and the like. We do have a picture of Mrs. Wilder when she presented the dolls to us.

Laura had brown pigtails and her bonnet is not on her head. Mary, of course, has her bonnet on.

This all happened in 1953, I think, when the tape was made of her answering questions that school children had sent in about Mary and the old bulldog, Jack. She noted some differences in the dolls and the way she characteristically remembered people—Almanzo and his buffalo coat being one thing in particular.

The buffalo coat must have reminded her of some things in Almanzo's life because she talked about the book *Farmer Boy* a little bit and said that it was true and that Almanzo's house was still standing.

LAURA'S GIFTS TO HER FRIENDS

Mrs. Wilder knew she was getting pretty frail. She once said to me, "I'm giving things to people that I think they will enjoy and take care of." She gave me her family Bible, the one her mother and father gave her when

Courtesy of Nava Austin

Mrs. Wilder and the dolls made for her by Barbara Brooks

she and Almanzo were married. The family Bible had clippings and obituaries in it, including one for their boy [died 1889, less than one month old]. I thought Rose was the only child they ever had because Mrs. Wilder herself never mentioned anything about a son.

It was a huge Bible, and there were obituaries for both her mother

and father. I'd never seen a Bible like it before, and she had pictures tucked away in it. If I am not mistaken, there was a paper clipping of when she and Almanzo got married. I had the Bible until they organized the home. Then Rose, her daughter, called and said, "I'm sure that Mother didn't know these things were going to be preserved." So, I told her yes I would give it back. The Bible is on display at the home; I gave it back to Mrs. Lichty who was curator then.

Mrs. Wilder gave away other things too, jewelry and the like, to people who had been good to her and who she thought would enjoy the items. She had quite a number of historical things that had been around for a long time.

She gave the library her books, which were mostly book club books. Evidently she had belonged to the Doubleday Book Club, and there may have been several other book clubs too. I would have thought there would have been more history books, but the books turned out to be mostly fiction books, mystery and western books and some bird books.

As she was giving away things, she also brought into the library Almanzo's canes, ones he had made himself, mostly from wood off the farm. One of them was made with several different kinds of wood. He had used a metal rod to run through the different pieces of cherry and oak to hold them together. Again, when the museum was set up, we gave those things back to them.

Not too long before she died she said that I was welcome to come to her home. "Anytime you come I'll let you in, but I'm not receiving guests at all. So many people are just curious to see what I look like." She wanted to be treated just as an individual, as a person, as a friend, not as a celebrity.

THE BOOKS SHE LOVED

She talked a lot about *Little House in the Big Woods* and her childhood life. And she also talked a lot about *The Long Winter* when her father and one of the neighbors went out to try to find food. That was when they had to burn straw for fuel. But *Little House in the Big Woods* was what she talked about more than anything.

In her later years she read mostly westerns. They were paperbacks. She said, "People probably wonder why this is my type of reading, but they are easy to hold, and I just enjoy them." And she was a horse lover, a lover of the outdoors. At one point, they had raised a colt. "I did the training of it," she said. But times were hard. It finally came to the fact that they had to sell the colt to pay the taxes on their home. That broke her heart.

Luke Short was one of her favorite western writers, and Mrs. Wilder had a lot of those old paperbacks that looked more like magazines than the paperbacks we have today. She gave me some of those, and I still have them. Zane Grey was another favorite.

Mrs. Wilder would feel pretty embarrassed about all of the fuss being made about her today. It is just not anything she ever would have wanted. She was a very feminine little lady, but she did enjoy receiving the letters from kids.

I did take Mrs. Wilder up on her invitation to visit just one time. She wanted some books, had run out of things to read, and couldn't get out. On that day, I picked up the books she had and took her some new ones, but I really didn't sit down and visit with her. But her little kitchen was very neat. Everything was real tidy. She said reading and playing solitaire were her livelihood.

I took her mostly westerns. She wasn't feeling well, and she could hold those books in bed and read. A hardcover book was almost too heavy

for her to hold, but she could relax with her westerns. I expect they reminded her somewhat of her past.

Now I never met Almanzo though I heard a lot about him. I was out that way the day he passed away. In fact, he had just passed away that morning, so I didn't stay or anything.

For some reason, Mrs. Wilder didn't talk about Rose much. I felt there may have been a little bit of a problem there. Her daughter didn't come often, and I don't think they were really close.

Mrs. Wilder and Rose were very different. Mrs. Wilder was very quiet and feminine, and Rose was more of the outgoing type. If Mrs. Wilder got help from Rose with her books, I never knew that.

Of course, Mrs. Wilder's books are still very popular. It is not only children; adults enjoy reading them. We have people who come back and say, "I've read them all two or three times, but I want to start them again."

When the TV show came along, I don't think it bothered people around here too much. They enjoyed [the television series], but they'd comment on the difference between the show and the stories. The show was far from her books, and it was far from picturing Mrs. Wilder. But it was just a show, I'd say, based on her books.

What Mrs. Wilder enjoyed doing was writing something that children would enjoy. She never figured on becoming famous. Nor was she the sort of person who felt that the old days were better. I think she was concerned about the economy and the country, but I never heard her say that she felt worried or unhappy about things either.

I don't remember her even complaining about growing older. She just accepted it as a phase of life. A lot of the time she wore a black velvet dress with a beautiful necklace. She was fond of jewelry but not overly fond. Toward the end of her years, children would write and say, "Why don't you

write more books?" She would reply, "I don't want to because I would have to bring in the sad things of life."

Most of her life was spent in the present and the future. To me, she had been just a friend, a personal friend.

CHAPTER 7

Volunteer for Life: The Personal Recollections of Irene V. Lichty

Irene and her husband, L. D. Lichty, were responsible for memorializing Laura Ingalls Wilder in her chosen setting. Their volunteer-led movement kept the idea of "doing something for Mrs. Wilder" alive. With the help of Laura's daughter, Rose Wilder Lane, they were able to preserve the main artifact of Mrs. Wilder's sixty-three years in the Ozarks: her home.

That home and part of the grounds that used to be Laura's Rocky Ridge Farm annually attract visitors from around the world who come to remember the woman they so admire in the setting she chose as her final stopping place. Once settled, she moved no more. Whatever wanderlust Laura still may have had was channeled into her homage to her Ingalls pioneer family: the eight books for which she is revered.

Mrs. Lichty came along late in Mrs. Wilder's earthly pilgrimage, but the convergence of their paths was fortuitous. Mrs. Lichty was the first curator of the Laura Ingalls Wilder Home and Museum and a driving force in its permanent establishment.

About twenty to thirty thousand tourists visit annually what is now the Laura Ingalls Wilder/Rose Wilder Lane Home and Museum; it is a number that has held steady for many years. Truthfully, some are a little disappointed that there isn't more to see, but Almanzo and Laura didn't live in a palace, just a ten-room house. Of course, most fans are just thrilled and satisfied to see the place. Somehow it is what they expected.

Certainly, the grounds haven't changed that much although there are fewer trees now than in years past. One year a terrible windstorm swept over the high Rocky Ridge hill and blew down a number of wonderful oak trees that were over a hundred years old. Laura and Almanzo were unhurt, the house untouched, but they received a number of letters of concern.

In having preserved Laura's home, Mrs. Lichty and her husband in

some sense preserved Laura too. For that, thousands are thankful. Of course, time stands still for no one. Mrs. Lichty passed away in 1993, full of the assurance she had preserved something truly worthwhile. SH

The friendship between Mrs. Wilder and me just sort of happened. I first met Mrs. Wilder—and I remember it very well—at a Methodist church ladies meeting. I noticed this nice-appearing lady who seemed to be getting a lot of attention. Everyone seemed so pleased that she was there. It turned out to be Mrs. Wilder, though I didn't know who she was at the time.

In some ways, we just kind of slipped into our friendship. She and my mother were also good friends, but I was the one who really got acquainted with her. I have never really known why the Lord made it so easy for us to do this.

Courtesy of James Lichty

Irene V. Lichty

Now, let's see . . . Almanzo was dead, so that would have been part of it. We were in Iowa when he passed away, but when we came back we would have been available and willing to take Mrs. Wilder places.

I got to know Rose quite well. Mrs. Wilder would ring me up and say, "Rose is here. Why don't you come out?" So we were together quite a little.

Mrs. Wilder owned a car but didn't drive it, so I would drive them around. I used to take them out to eat at a popular place down highway 60 beyond Mountain Grove. One day after

we left there, I don't quite know what happened, but I screwed up a little bit in my driving. I didn't have accidents, but I must have pulled over on the shoulder. Rose didn't exactly jump; just appeared a little frightened. Mrs. Wilder herself never seemed the least bit nervous about my driving.

Springfield News-Leader

Signing books at age 84

At the time of Mr. Wilder's death, as I understand, she hadn't been very involved in church things. Her mode of living had changed somewhat and she wasn't so active. But during the time that I knew her, if I invited her to a meeting, she seemed happy to come. I guess she was more involved in her thinking than her activities would show.

"She was friendly to everyone. Yet... when a person becomes famous, even their friends become a little standoffish."

I feel that Mrs. Wilder did have quite a few acquaintances—and many people who wanted to get acquainted with her. I don't think there was any discrimination on her part; it's just that she had only so much time and strength. She had to be a little careful.

One day I did take her into Springfield. She had been invited there to autograph books in the store. That event went on all afternoon. I knew she was getting tired, so before she got too worn out, I said to the lady running the store, "I believe that is as far as she should go."

When I left her at her home, she got out and said, "I'm quite tired but I had a good time!"

Mrs. Wilder never had television, did lots of reading, and had wide interests. She was friendly to everyone. Yet it is so often that when a person becomes famous, even their friends become a little standoffish. They may feel like this person is beyond knowing me now. I know that Mrs. Wilder would not have wanted any of her friends to feel that way.

Blue was her outstanding color, and she wore hats. Those were the days of hats. Mrs. Wilder liked most anything to eat, and she always seemed to enjoy what she had at our place, just because it was different and because she was eating with different people instead of eating alone.

Mrs. Wilder was modern in her thinking. She kept up on politics and was a staunch Democrat, though slipping a little. She would probably think it was all right for women to go outside the home to work. She was the same person when we met her, I'm sure, that she had been for years.

THE FOUNDING OF THE LAURA INGALLS WILDER HOME AND MUSEUM

Like my getting to know Mrs. Wilder, the founding of the home just sort of happened. My husband, L. D. Lichty, was around the house, and he said to me, "Has anyone ever said anything to you about honoring Mrs. Wilder?" I said, "No, there's never been anything said about it to me."

Then I told my husband I was going to a club meeting and would mention the idea if it worked out naturally. When I did everyone seemed to pick up on it. They knew what sort of person she was and how important she was to Mansfield, but they hadn't seemed to have thought about doing anything to honor her. All I did was start a little talking and thinking about it.

In fact, that reminds me that a woman from Ava, a town which I think was a little larger than Mansfield back then, said to me, "If we had had the Wilders down in Ava, we would have done something for her before

this." I thought to myself, *That's true. Ava would have.* So it took awhile for Mansfield to wake up to the opportunity.

None of this happened while Mrs. Wilder was living. She would have been embarrassed. For a time, things developed in a casual way. It was not the sort of thing that could be pushed.

When Rose finally understood what we were wanting to do with the home, I could tell that she was pleased about it. She said, "Well, if you want to do something, I'd be glad to help." I don't think she jumped into things because, you know, in small places and in large places too, there is often someone there ready to take personal advantage.

I do recall that when the announcement was made, perhaps in the paper, that there would be an organizational meeting for anyone interested in furthering "the cause," well, the word got out some way that there was money to be distributed. That was never true. When people found out at the meeting that that wasn't so, some of them were not interested anymore.

Actually, the real opening of the house didn't take place until quite some time after Mrs. Wilder passed away. As I remember, the first time the home was open for people to look at, was when a ladies club showed some interest. So, one Sunday afternoon, people were allowed to go into the home. Enough people were there to keep an eye on things and know what was going on.

I'm afraid we never opened the upstairs. The stairway was a little treacherous. If one person went up, another person would want to also, and they wouldn't understand why you couldn't allow it.

I must say that it was some of my husband's money that took care of some things. There wasn't a lot of expense to start with; we did what came up to do. We did not charge admission at first, and that was foolish. I believe

it was Rose who suggested that we had better charge admission because a lot of people were coming out of curiosity.

People came from all over the world: England, Germany, and Japan. Most were from Europe. I don't remember anyone from the TV show ever coming by. We had a guest book and sometimes people would write their names down. We wouldn't know for sure who they were, and we didn't quiz anyone.

CHAPTER 8

Friends and Neighbors: The Personal Recollections of Mrs. Iola Jones, Sheldon Jones, and Roscoe Jones

The Jones family lived just down the road from the Wilders, away from town and off to the right as you go out past the Wilder home itself. Marvin Jones moved his family there right after World War II to tackle the rough land. He worked at a service station and farmed on the side, a prudent thing for an Ozark farmer to do.

For the children, the farm was mostly a great place to grow up and learn responsibility. The Jones boys, Sheldon and Roscoe, worked; everybody worked. Neither of the boys farms now, however. They learned that farming was good for their character but bad for their pocketbooks.

Farming was good for their character but bad for their pocketbooks.

All the Joneses left the farm in 1957, though not before Marvin was a pallbearer at Mrs. Wilder's funeral. After a time in Joplin, Sheldon and Roscoe took up trucking. They live in the Springfield, Missouri, area now.

First we'll hear from Iola Jones, the boys' mother. SH

IOLA JONES

My husband was in the service and got home around '46. We built a house that was just east of the Wilders on the same side of the road, not toward town but away from town. E. R. Smith built a house in between ours and the Wilders but that was much later.

The boys were over there more than I was. I was real busy, and her husband was living at that time. But it was not long after we moved there that he died.

I'd just go see her sometimes. I'd send her some cookies or something by the kids. I think one time the St. Louis paper interviewed her and said that she made cookies for the neighbor boys. But she said, "That's not what I said! I said the neighbor boys 'brought' me cookies." They were rolled sugar cookies or oatmeal cookies.

When you went to visit her privately she was pretty talkative, but she wasn't that way in a crowd. She was very quiet. But to go over and visit her, no. She always had a list of little quotations or sayings or poems that she kept in her head. Sometimes I would know them; sometimes I didn't. She was just real entertaining to visit with, and such a cute little woman.

On my fortieth birthday, I walked up to the Wilder home. I told Mrs. Wilder that I guessed that life had just begun for me, since they say, "Life begins at forty."

"No, dearie," Mrs. Wilder said, "life begins at eighty."

"No, dearie," Mrs. Wilder said, "life begins at eighty."

She was always asking about my boys, Sheldon and Roscoe. She didn't think they would ever do anything bad. One time when I was over she told me, "Sheldon will be over here and I will think: *it must be Sheldon that I love the best.* Then, in a day or so, Roscoe will come and then I'll think: *Oh, no. It must be Roscoe that I love the best.*" She really was crazy about the boys.

When the boys would visit her, they were so interested in life back then, they would ask her all kinds of questions about life in her books. She loved to talk about that, of course. And they liked to hear it.

The teacher used to read these books at school, and I used to read [them to the boys] a lot after chores were done, supper was over, and the dishes were done and the fire was revved up for the evening.

I remember one night they brought home a book that the teacher had already read to them. I hadn't read the book, and the boys were sitting on either side of me. I said, "Now, I'm going to finish this one chapter, and you go to bed." But it was kind of exciting, so I too wanted to see what happened next. "Just one more chapter, just one more," the boys said.

Then one of them started to say what was going to happen in the chapter we were reading, and the other one said, "Oh, let mother be surprised."

"You've already read this!" I said. "Oh, yes," they said. But those books were so interesting they wanted me to read, read, read.

Once she asked the boys which one was their favorite. Sheldon liked *Farmer Boy*, so she gave him that autographed for Christmas. Roscoe liked *The Long Winter*, and she gave him that. I wish we could have afforded a complete set for both of them, but we couldn't afford that. They must have been $2.75 a book.

Just south of the Wilder house is a spring, and terrapins used to come up from this spring to the back porch where the screen came down way low. In the evenings those terrapins got so that they would line up and look in. Then Mrs. Wilder would fix bread in milk and feed them as they stretched out their necks. I've never seen anything like it.

Of course, they had their own animals—milk goats. And they were always able to keep them in. In fact, the Wilder fence came right up to our yard, and our kids would feed the goats. I used to warn them that the one billy goat would come over that fence after them, but it never did.

Mrs. Wilder was always doing things for people, sending them things, like birthday cards she would write to you. I would send her some of my light bread, homemade bread made with regular flour. I don't think they had whole wheat flour back then. If they did, we didn't use it.

She'd also eat an awful lot of fruit. She believed in eating the right things. I remember being there when they brought the groceries in, lots of grapefruit, bananas, and oranges, and she'd cook. She'd make soup.

So far as dress goes, she dressed old-fashion-like. She had nice clothes, but they were clothes she had had a long time. When she went to church, she was real old-fashioned, lace around her neck. I remember she had one dark maroon velvet dress, which she wore at the library dedication when it

was named after her. I've got a napkin from that time with the date written on it.

Of course, she had done sewing earlier in her life, but at the time I knew her she didn't do that. Instead, she read a lot and had lots of mail.

Sometimes the mail would get to be too much and she'd have her hands full. Sometimes Roscoe would help her with it, sometimes Sheldon. At her age, I don't think she could respond to it all.

"She talked about how she would make word pictures for Mary so she could 'see.'"

She spent a lot of time just sitting in a chair right by the dining room table. We'd find her there when we went over. Once in a while we would sit on the swing on the porch, but not too often. When she wanted to show you something, she would jump right up and take off. She didn't have arthritis, and she got around fast.

She used to talk about her family of long ago. Especially I remember her talking about the sister who was blind. That was Mary. And she talked about how she would make word pictures for Mary so she could "see." She was a special companion to Mary and had lots of feeling for her.

Mary's organ was there in the home, but I don't know whether Mrs. Wilder played it or not.

Mrs. Wilder had a good sense of humor and lots of wisdom, really; and she put it across in such an interesting way. She had been quite active in her church. In fact, she went to church with me quite a lot, which was a pickup in her activity because before that she hadn't been going. You see, I don't think she ever drove, so I think Almanzo's death kept her in.

She did talk about spiritual things, and we went together to the Methodist Church where she had always gone. I can remember her telling me one time that she had memorized a book of the Bible, but I don't remember which one. She just didn't talk about herself a lot.

I would say that Rose was not the same type of person as her mother.

Of course, she had traveled a lot and was real interesting to visit with. She'd come from Danbury, Connecticut, to visit her mother, but she didn't stay very long. I remember Mrs. Wilder as being sort of stylish, and her hair was gray and always fixed up. By comparison Rose didn't seem that refined.

I am sure Mrs. Wilder had a lot of money. Sheldon was saying to me that one time when he was over there helping with the stacks of mail, she remarked that she needed to go to the bank; the money had gotten to be a chore. There was about $6,000 on that table.

When we visited the Laura Ingalls Wilder Home, the place seemed pretty much the same except that there were fewer trees, and they had changed the driveway. When Mrs. Wilder died, my husband was a pallbearer. You know, I have the little memorial of her funeral service, but I don't even remember the hymns that we sang. That was a long time ago.

SHELDON JONES

Sheldon Jones picks up where his mother has left off. He has only recently been reminded of Mrs. Wilder. He too has been to the Home and Museum but came away dissatisfied. His memory is almost too good, and he is disquieted about inaccuracies that tend to crop up when people who never knew the Wilders attempt to explain how they lived or, specifically, how Mrs. Wilder lived toward the end of her life.

Though he was only a young boy during Mrs. Wilder's later years, he had a keen eye for details, which he now shares with enthusiasm and obvious enjoyment. It takes little prompting for him to remember those days. SH

Only last night, I was talking about working for her. And if I wasn't working for her, I'd run by and see about her. You see, until Almanzo

died they were pretty much loners. In fact, I never saw him, not one time to speak of. He must have been sort of like her dad. You might be twenty miles away, but you were still too close. He didn't deal with people; at that time he had little to do with them. Now she, Mrs. Wilder, was quite a lady.

I really got to going over there after he died. Then she needed help. But the house really wasn't open for visitors. There were always people coming by in the summertime wanting to meet her. I don't know how many times I'd be working in the yard when I'd have to make a run for the back door to get between visitors and the house.

They'd say, "We want to meet Mrs. Wilder." They'd come from Iowa, Nebraska, and, of course, Missouri and Kansas and way off states and even foreign countries. And I'd have to say, "No, no, no. It's not that she is uppity or anything, but she won't be coming to the door; she won't meet you. It's not that she's so important or nothing, but the reason I am here is this is as far as it goes."

I told a lot of people that. You know, a kid standing there telling you that, wouldn't you like to knock him down? But I felt like I was protecting her. I knew that was what she wanted because there would be times when people would come, and she'd be at the door herself saying, "Thanks for coming, but no . . ."

At that time, she just didn't want to get out much. I think Ma and I and Roscoe and Virginia Hartley and a few others were about the only ones she saw.

So, I took her the mail and mowed the yard with a power mower. Actually, there were push mowers for quite a while. I mowed her yard and the yard of the folks that had bought land out there from her.

I was out there raking one day during the fall when it was extremely

windy. I was battling like crazy when she came out and said, "Aren't you fighting it? We'll consider it two days' work."

I was telling Mom last night that the driveway is all changed now. It made a sweeping circle, then came down to the road, the opposite of the way it is now. But I'd go down and rake that gravel because it would wash out. She wanted it raked in such a way that the gravel would be heaped back where it belonged. She wanted sort of a mound of gravel so it wouldn't wash the driveway away.

Sometimes that is about all I got done there. Then I would put up the tools. She was a real stickler for putting up the tools exactly where Almanzo had hung them, I suppose because they were placed right there by him and everything was hung up. He spent his lifetime taking care of his tools, and she knew where they went.

Mrs. Wilder gave me a quarter for that work. That was big money for a kid. I imagine when she was a kid you'd work maybe for a penny, and she must have pinched pennies all her life.

Mrs. Wilder probably didn't realize what she had. I don't know what kind of money they had before the books, but they must have lived modestly. I'm sure he was an ace farmer from what I gathered from her. But she had a big table maybe three and a half feet across. No, maybe not that big. I'd be there to visit her, and there would be a pile of money on the table, checks and money, maybe four inches high.

Why she had the money I don't know. Royalties wouldn't have come that way; but if she was going to write me something, she'd push that pile back out of the way. It was aggravating; money was a nuisance. She told my brother one time, "This must get to the bank; this is such an aggravation!" I suppose Hartley could have taken her to town. But she didn't leave; she didn't get out much.

Once I went out to the house with my daughter, who was four or five. And this young lady, maybe she was from New York or Pennsylvania or something, led us around; and she had a little story, but it was all wrong from what I remembered. The more she talked, the more irritable I got.

Herbert Hoover Presidential Library

Mrs. Wilder's modern Ozark kitchen

Finally, she came to Mrs. Wilder's parlor where she had kept all her books, and she said, "This is where Mrs. Wilder entertained all her guests." Then I said, "No, young lady, that is not right. This room was kept closed."

You see, that parlor was kept dark, never used. Many a time I would go in there during the winter and take all the books out and lay them around and turn on electric heaters to dry them out. It was damp in there and dark, and it was never heated.

The young lady was taken aback, but said maybe Mrs. Wilder could have entertained guests there. Of course, I don't know about the years before we knew her as to what she did. But I interrupted at another point and said, "No, no. There's not a word of truth to that." So, one guy said, "Did you know her?"

I said, "I worked for her when I was a kid for several years. During the summertime my brother and I would go in here and move these heavy old drapes and open the windows, and it would air out all day. The doors would be opened up, everything. And then before I left that evening the windows would be closed, the drapes pulled, and the door closed. It stayed dark, and she never went in there."

That was the room that had the fireplace. She lived basically in the dining room, kitchen, and bedroom. That was it, because I remember seeing her once in that little screened-in porch that is just off the dining room. Mrs. Wilder and Mom used to go out there and sit, and one day I saw them there. I remember it because it was so unusual to see anybody there.

The only time I ever remember even seeing Mr. Wilder was while we were bailing hay. We hayed all around that place, and he didn't even speak then. I couldn't tell you what he looked like because he mostly stayed in the house too.

I don't think Mrs. Wilder realized what she had created in her books. I think she was just writing down memories at the time, just sketching, just thinking about the past. For somebody to really get excited about it—how did she put that to me one time? "What do you see in them?" she asked.

My gosh! I would have loved to live in those times!

I was always asking her about her books and what kind of life she led. She was truthful in her books, but she was always cautious about who she named and how she showed them. I remember her talking about that

mean girl, Nellie. Of course, that wasn't her real name, but I remember Mrs. Wilder saying that she didn't put her down nearly as mean as she was.

When she talked about Pa, Ma, and Mary, it was pretty much in line with the books. Her dad's attitude was, if he could see smoke coming from a chimney, he didn't have to see the chimney. People were too close; they'd move on. I remember she mentioned the moving.

Mrs. Wilder . . . didn't put [Nellie] down nearly as mean as she was.

Mrs. Wilder thought her bulldog, an old boxer with some black color around one eye, was the greatest thing that walked around on four legs. He had the rule of the place. You'd come in the house, and he'd come out of the bedroom and go straight upstairs from the kitchen, straight up. It was some sort of escape in case of fire.

If the dog didn't want to bother with you, he never got up. He just lay there in a corner. But a lot of times that sucker would come up slobbering and lay his head right in your lap! That dog got killed on the highway that runs by the place. It really hurt Mrs. Wilder bad.

One time I was sitting there with Mrs. Wilder after dark. I liked most animals, and she had a big cat that was sitting on my lap. Mrs. Wilder was sitting over at the table where she always sat. I was petting the cat, playing with him, and I got to teasing him. I didn't think Mrs. Wilder could see me. The cat was sitting in my lap, and I would blow in his face. You know how they don't like that. He'd lay back his ears, and snarl at me, just mad enough to kill, and then I'd pet him and it would be over with. Then I'd go do it to him again.

I tell you, all of a sudden, that old tom cat took a swipe at me and jumped off my lap. I said, "What's the matter, cat?" She said, "He wouldn't do that if you wouldn't pick on him." She'd seen it all!

Mrs. Wilder was something. She was a real lady, absolutely a real lady.

ROSCOE JONES

Roscoe Jones runs a trucking company and a portable phone is ever with him. Although running such an operation calls for travel, he is surprised how seldom he goes to Mansfield, fifty miles east of Springfield, where he now lives.

Roscoe was nine years old when Almanzo died. Both of the Jones "boys" have a great capacity for recalling detail, but they wish they remembered more of their neighbor. To them, she was just that—very interesting to talk to and convenient to do odd jobs for, but not a celebrity. That term would have been foreign to them. They make clear that Mrs. Wilder never considered herself a celebrity either and avoided the limelight if at all possible.

Whereas Sheldon has spoken with a sense of narrative to his reminiscences, Roscoe's style is clipped and direct, possibly because I talked with him over lunch in the midst of a rushed day. SH

Pretty much what Sheldon and I did for her was seasonal chores. When it started turning cold, she always wanted a bale of straw broken and put back under the areas of the house to close the vents to make it airtight.

That was it basically. Sometimes she would have something in the house to move. One day she called me and asked me to come over and move some stuff for her. At that time, she gave me her old typewriter, which I still have. I hauled it home on my motor scooter.

Really we didn't get to know Mrs. Wilder until Mr. Wilder died. As boys we would have never gone up there on our own because he seemed like a grouchy old man. I do remember seeing him a few times. He would come out into the yard when we would drive up.

When he died I began mowing her yard. We always had a power mower, but you had to push it. It was a big, big job.

Really, Mrs. Wilder was a very, very kind person and a real sweet lady. She used to call and have us pick up her mail when she couldn't do it. That driveway must have been rather steep to her.

Sometimes she just wanted to visit with someone. She used to tell us the same stories she wrote about in her books. Then she'd say, "Well, now this is the way this story actually happened." She would say that some of the book, I forget the term she used, was more "flowery" or something to "jazz it up," although I am certain she wouldn't use that term.

I don't remember her ever saying that she had a favorite story. She talked very fondly of her family and about all of the hard times they had gone through.

No, she never went through the house to point out any items of special interest. I do recall being fascinated by some sort of apparatus she had in her library. It had a light with a colored lens of some sort on it that was used to dry out books or keep down the humidity level. I mentioned that when I was down at the home a few years ago, but no one else seemed to know about it.

I don't think Mrs. Wilder had too much of a fancy for fine furnishings. In fact, I don't ever remember her talking about things.

But she liked to talk, and she had a sense of humor; she surely did. When she received candy in the mail, I don't know where it came from, maybe the publisher, she would have Sheldon and me over. She would get boxes of chocolates and that was sort of a rare thing for us at that time.

In dress, Mrs. Wilder was old fashioned. She wore long dresses around the house with a sweater and maybe a shawl and laced-up boots. Nothing fancy. Actually, she didn't even have a couch in the room where the stove

was. She sat in a rocking chair, and there may have been a side chair or two, just straight wooden chairs.

Possibly Mr. Wilder made the chairs. I don't know. I am sure that Mrs. Wilder did not sell off his tools. I don't remember if they sold them off after she died or not.

Mr. Wilder made toy wagons the size of coaster wagons. His were quite unique because the bed of the wagon was made to look more like that of a full-sized wagon. It had larger wheels on the rear than on the front. These wagons were always fascinating to me, and I have no idea what became of them. Of course, the old shop is gone, but I've been told by other people that he was quite a handyman. I don't know why or for whom he made those wagons.

Virginia Hartley was probably her closest friend of long standing. Virginia's father-in-law had a taxi service and I do remember him coming out whenever the Wilders wanted to go someplace. I remember it was a green Oldsmobile.

However, she did come to rely on Mother quite a bit and developed a fairly close relationship with her in the years we lived there. And Mother provided a ride for her to get started going back to church. Before that I don't think she had been there for years. She did come to feel free to call Mother for things she might need. Yes, they were fairly close.

Mother and daughter were not so close, I think. I remember meeting Rose on two or three occasions, and she was there for her mother's funeral. Rose would come to visit for a week or two at a time, and she wasn't nearly as easy to visit with as her mother because she seemed so brash.

I'm not sure they got along too well. They seemed to tolerate each other while Rose visited. I even remember Mrs. Wilder saying that she was not looking forward to her upcoming visit with Rose.

Now the Harland Shorters had business dealings with both of them, I think. Harland is my uncle and now lives in Florida. He was the one who told me Mr. Wilder had sort of a club foot.

The Shorters first bought Rose's farm, the one with the stone house, and lived there for a number of years. Then they bought the Wilder place itself. Gerida, Harland's wife, was my father's sister.

When they bought the Wilder farm, I believe it was contracted so that Mrs. Wilder could live in her home for as long as she wanted. Once she passed away, then all of that became the Shorters' property. It was a large farm for that day and time and area.

The dairy was over on Rose's old place; the Shorters had cattle. Actually, the Wilder farm had little tillable land. The open field between our house and theirs would have been about the only place you could use for hay. There was very little flat land, but then, of course, there is very little flat land in Wright County!

CHAPTER 9

World War I: As Seen by Laura Ingalls Wilder in the *Missouri Ruralist*

During Laura Ingalls Wilder's Mansfield years, major world events began to intrude on the life of her beloved town. Someone called an archduke was assassinated in an obscure place called Sarajevo, Bosnia. An equally obscure country called Austria-Hungary then declared war on its neighbor country Serbia, blaming it for the political conditions that led to the archduke's assassination.

Then, one-by-one, the great powers became involved in the conflict through their treaty obligations to one another. Finally, Germany took the opportunity provided by a disintegrating Europe and invaded neutral Belgium and then France. Britain declared war on Germany. World War I had begun. Before its end some twenty million people were dead.

I feel sure Mrs. Wilder would have preferred to tend her chickens, cook the farm meals, and watch the seasons come and go at her beloved Rocky Ridge Farm rather than become a commentator on world events; but the "Great War," the "war to end all wars," could not be pushed aside.

Along with the majority of other Americans, Laura felt a strong sense of moral outrage about the war. Germany was particularly guilty of great moral wrongs. As war fever eventually seized even America, Laura came to feel that Germany had broken basic Christian principles by disregarding her promises not to invade Belgium. There were weekly reports in the news about German "atrocities."

When America finally declared war itself, ordinary farm work suddenly took on new meaning. Mere commercial gain and self-betterment were no longer the main features of daily life. Now good crops and determined thrift became weapons in the war between good and evil. No one was insignificant in this battle; mundane everyday activities took on heroic aspects. Even farmers could be a key to victory. No wonder Mrs. Wilder

agreed with the young man who exclaimed: "Glory! What days in which to live!"

In this chapter are a number of Mrs. Wilder's regular columns in the *Missouri Ruralist* in which she talks about the war and its effects on farmers, Mansfield, America, and the world. SH

Victory May Depend on You

February 20, 1918

"It is a war in each man's heart. Each man is fighting as the spirit moves him," said Hira Singh, speaking of the war, in the absorbing story of Talbot Mundy.

Every day is showing more plainly that Hira Singh was right and that his statement is true in more ways than the author meant. It is a fact that not only is it a "war in each man's heart," but that the issues of this war are being fought over in the hearts of all the people—men, women and children.

The keynote of the statement of the nation's war aims, made by President Wilson recently, was unselfishness, an unselfish championing of the rights of nations too small to defend themselves and of people who have been oppressed so long they are helpless.

As a nation we stand for unselfishness, courage, and self-sacrifice in defense of the right. Our soldiers are fighting on the battlefields that these principles shall be recognized as governing the nations of the world. And our hearts are the battlefields where these same qualities strive to become rulers of our actions.

It is indeed a "war in each man's heart," and as the battles go in these hearts of ours so will be the victory or defeat of the armies in the field, for a nation can be no greater than the sum of the greatness of its people. There never before has been a war where the action of each individual had such a direct bearing on the whole world.

One of the liveliest skirmishes of which I know takes place when our spirit of patriotism and duty comes in conflict with our instinct of

hospitality, for here a seeming generosity to those near at hand blinds us to the fact that in these days when we feed those who are not hungry we are stealing from those who are starving, even though the food is our own.

We are all in the habit of feeding our friends when we entertain them and we feel we have failed as hosts if we do not offer our guests the usual feast of good things. Now is our opportunity to substitute for this the "feast of reason and the flow of soul" which is the only thing that makes the meeting of friends worthwhile. Now is our chance to see that the food and the companionship are placed in their proper relation to each other, with the food, of course, secondary.

The refreshments at an evening gathering during the holidays were brown bread sandwiches and coffee. The entertainment is an annual affair and although elaborate refreshments always were served in previous years, the evening was a bigger success this year than ever before.

What the War Means to Women

May 5, 1918

"This is a woman's war and the women will see to it that before the war is ended the world shall be made safe for women." This sentiment was expressed by a woman in my hearing soon after the declaration of war by the United States.

"This is a woman's war."

Every war is more or less a woman's war, God knows, but is this in an especial way a woman's war? Never before in the history of the world has war been deliberately made upon the womanhood of the world. Motherhood, woman's crown and glory, has been made her scourge and shame. The tortures by savages, tales of which used to make our blood run cold did not equal in horror and cruelty what has been inflicted upon educated, refined women and ignorant peasant women alike.

Stripped naked and driven along the roads out of their own country is a sport for drunken soldiery. Thrown by the hundreds into the rivers when the crowds of soldiers had tired of them—this was a part of the war in Armenia.

Death by the thousands, after nameless horrors and suffering, takes place along the roads of Poland!

Driven over the snow covered mountains of Serbia—dying of hunger and exhaustion and wounds, a fate preferred to falling into the hands of the invaders—this was the fate of the women of Serbia.

Women are tortured and defiled, mutilated and murdered in Belgium and northern France! The mind revolts and the soul sickens at even trying to contemplate the things that women have been made to suffer by Germany's invading armies.

There has been a planned, deliberate attempt, by the enemy, to destroy the other nations of the world. To destroy a nation, its women and children must be exterminated and so a part of this incredible plot has been to so mutilate and destroy the women of those nations that they will bear no more children to perpetuate their race.

All over the world women are bravely taking their part in the conflict and doing what they can to defend those things they hold most sacred, their homes, their children and their honor. In all the allied countries women are filling places of responsibility and danger, doing hard, unpleasant work to help in the struggle to "make the world safe for women."

The Bettman Archive

A brigade of women soldiers being prepared for frontline action

Women are showing their fearlessness on all the battle fronts. In Russia when the soldiers refused to fight, the women formed the famous "Battalion of Death" and met the enemy on the first line. They held their section of the line, too, when on every side the soldiers retreated in disorder and though every woman in the battalion was killed or wounded. Later, with their ranks refilled, this battalion of women took part in the fighting at Petrograd, defending their position dauntlessly, seemingly without fear of death.

The women in the Red Cross units on the western front hesitate at nothing they find to do to help the allied cause. They were the last to leave the abandoned towns before the Germans entered; and they helped the

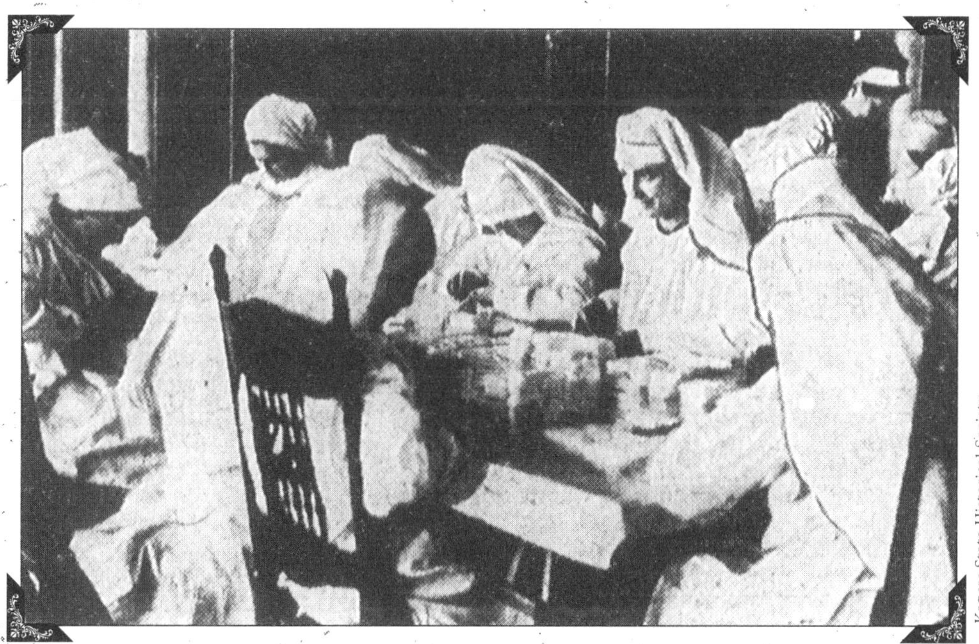

Kansas State Historical Society

Making bandages for the Red Cross

refugees to escape; picked up and removed scores of wounded, driving their own trucks and motor cars; established temporary kitchens near the front to feed the soldiers who had not eaten for hours; and when the emergency arose, took charge of the military traffic and directed the columns of guns, cavalry, supply wagons and troops and prevented a traffic jam.

The women of the American Red Cross are winning honor on the western battle front. They act as cooks or chauffeurs, traffic policemen, stretcher bearers or grave diggers as the occasion arises.

Women in sheltered America have perhaps been slow to realize what the war means to them but they are beginning to understand. Among them, as among the men, are some pessimists and whiners, also some cowards and slackers, but they are few.

When the British retreated on the west, the first of April, a man remarked, "They're licking the stuffing out of us, licking us every day," and a woman answered, "What does one retreat amount to? A man isn't whipped in a fight even if he is knocked down, if he just gets up and comes again."

I like the spirit of the man whom I heard say, "We can't be whipped! We won't be whipped! We'll fight for 60 years if we must, but we'll never give up!"

A widow whose son volunteered and is now in France, said she was so proud of him that she had no time to be sorry, that she was glad he had gone and could not understand how any young man could stay at home.

Another woman, speaking of her son who had volunteered, said she was proud of him and that he would have been ashamed to look his sister in the face if he had not gone to help protect her from the fate of the girls of Belgium and France.

The congregation at the church was remarkable on Easter Sunday for the absence of new hats and the large number of Liberty Bond pins and Red

Cross buttons. One woman who has always taken great pride in her apparel said to me: "I can't get a new hat this summer. I'm paying for my Liberty Bond and helping with the Red Cross, and someway new hats don't seem to matter."

The little town of Mansfield and the immediate vicinity oversubscribed its quota in the Third Liberty Loan.

How About the Home Front?

May 20, 1918

When we buy Liberty Bonds and War Savings Stamps, we're open to suspicion, in our own minds at least, of not being entirely disinterested. We may be a little influenced in our saving and buying by a hope of gain, for Liberty Bonds and Savings Stamps are good investments. They are gilt-edged securities and a paying proposition.

Even when we work hard on our farms raising food to "feed the world" we are making money for ourselves and the harder we work the more we make, so perhaps we do not deserve so very much credit for the extra effort after all. We are such complex creatures and our motives are nearly always so mixed, that it is easy to deceive ourselves. I know from experience that it is very pleasant to have duty and inclination run hand in hand and to be well paid in cash for doing right.

When we give to the Red Cross, however, it is entirely different. What we give them we do not make a profit on, at least in money. We get nothing in return except a glow of satisfaction and a knowledge that we are actually helping our soldiers at the front and the ill and destitute of the world.

By the sacrifice we make in giving, we show our love for humanity, our pity for the helpless, and our generosity toward those less fortunate than ourselves.

It is something of which to be very proud when one's community goes over its allotment for the Red Cross as so many have done. It is another victory over the enemy, for this war is a battle of ideas and standards of life.

Disguise it as we may in concrete terms such as "the restoration of Belgium," the "rights of small nations" and the "integrity of treaties," this world war is a world conflict of ideas. This is why the fighting cannot be confined to the battle fronts, why every country is more or less in conflict internally. We are in the midst of a battle of standards of conduct and each of us is a soldier in the ranks. What we do and how we live our everyday lives has a direct bearing on the result, just as each of us will be personally affected by it.

We may have thought that a little selfishness and over-reaching on our part, a breaking of our promised word now and then if it was more convenient, a disregard of the rights of others for our own advantage, did not so much matter and were not so very wrong. Nevertheless it is these same things when done in mass by the German government and armies, that the remainder of the world abhors.

There is a connection between our motives, the way we live our lives here at home, and those vast armies facing each other in a death grapple.

In the thick of battle, under terrific bombardments that shake the earth, in the darkness of night when the poison gas comes creeping, our soldiers are fighting that right shall be the standard of the future instead of might, that the strong shall not take unfair advantage of the weak, that a pledged word and honor shall be considered sacred and shall not be broken.

Are we fighting bravely for these same things all down the line? When "Johnny comes marching home" victorious will he find that we also have won the victory on the home front?

If we are careless of our given word, if we take unfair advantage; if we are deceitful and lustful and cruel, if we spread false reports, if we are malicious and grasping and full of hate instead of kind, open-minded, fair,

and just, then the Prussian ideas, as insidious as their poison gas, will have vanquished in our own country those ideals for which our armies fight.

This is our battle and must be our victory, for if the standards of life approved by the German government hold the people of the earth, then, in a different way than was intended but in a very true sense, Germany will have conquered the world.

Are You Helping or Hindering?

July 5, 1918

A "government of the people, for the people and by the people" can be no better nor greater than the people.

My friend had been telling me a tale of graft and injustice in relatively high places and she concluded with, "And this is a government of the people, for the people, by the people." If we could point to no such instances among those more or less in power, it would very plainly not be a government representative of the people, for there are good, bad, and indifferent persons among the people and a few who make mistakes now and then.

From town constable to the chief executive, we find good officers, bad officers, and those who are negligible, for the people are the government and the government is the people. If we want the one perfect, we must reform the other for I will venture to say that if there were no dishonesty, or grafting, or self-seeking among the rank and file of the people, there would be none in any department of government.

I knew of one person in the recent Red Cross drive who bought as cheaply as possible at a Red Cross auction and resold at a profit. There were only a few dollars involved but there was the soul of a profiteer in a person with small means who, though at the bottom of the social structure financially, is just as obnoxious as the man who makes millions out of the suffering of the world.

Not far from this man lives another who served in the U.S. army all through the Spanish war and who has never been in good health since. He is entitled to a pension but never has applied for one because, in his

own words, he "could make a livin'." He told me the other day when we happened to meet, that just before the United States went into this war he had decided to ask for his pension but had not done so when war was declared. He said, "Then I told my wife that the government would have lots of expenses without paying me a pension, and we talked it over and decided that we would not ask for a pension until this mess was straightened out and government expenses were lighter. Then I'd be older if I was alive and I'd ask for a pension. If I was dead my wife could get one. Oh! I wish I could turn things back and be young enough; I'd go and fight!"

This man is just as much a self-sacrificing patriot as George Washington, though just a humble wood cutter like the great Lincoln. Then between the two extremes of patriotism and slackerism are numbers of indifferently good patriots sacrificing a little, doing the greater part of their duty by their country.

I have heard people who have been inoculated with I. W. W. [Industrial Workers of the World] doctrine say "if this government don't do right, we will turn it over." If it were turned over, we would have on top what had before been the bottom and we would perhaps have in power both the man who made money from the Red Cross sale and the one who is going without his pension to help his country, though I'll wager the moneymaker would scheme himself into some place where the graft pickings were good.

We have no king in a republic "who can do no wrong," no kaiser whom we are bound to regard as infallible with the right to both our minds and our bodies, but from the lowest to the highest we are bound by the same standards; we are sworn to the same ideals and permeated alike with good and evil and all alike we are liable to make mistakes.

When we are tempted to be impatient and too critical of our leaders, we might think as I heard a woman say, "few of us would have their jobs." Friendly, constructive criticism is one thing, and unkind, nagging fault-finding is another quite different.

Imagine a man fighting, for his life and the lives of his friends, and while he is struggling to the limit of his strength, his friends stand around and cry: "Oh that was wrong! You shouldn't have hit him on the nose; you should have landed on his jaw!" "Why did you let him hit you? If you had been quicker you could have stopped him. You're too slow!" "You ought not to have taken that drink this morning! Stop now and tell us! Will you be a teetotaler after this?" "Hey! This fellow in the crowd is stepping on my toes! Make him quit!" "You never can lick him for you weren't trained. You should have been prepared for this!"

Wouldn't that man fight better if he were encouraged by cries of, "That's a good one! Hit him again! You've got him going now; keep after him!" and so forth? If the principle is good in a game of ball, why not use it in this bigger game? Let's root for our leaders now and then!

I would like to read, for instance, that Congress had called Secretary Baker into its presence and said to him, "Well done, Secretary Baker! It is a remarkable achievement to transport so many troops safely to France in so short a time, and we honor you for it."

Instead of so much wailing because we must eat cornbread, I would like to hear someone say, "What a wonderful man Mr. Hoover is to be able to regulate the food supply of the world; to handle the food of our country so that we may not come to hunger and perhaps famine and still are able to feed other nations!"

Let's talk to each other about the ideals of life and government that President Wilson is putting before the world! If we, the people, hold fast to

and live by these beautiful ideals, they are bound to be enacted by our government for, in a republic, the ideas of the people reach upward to the top instead of being handed down from someone at the top to the people who must accept them whether they like them or not.

Keep the Saving Habit

March 20, 1919

"We may have all the sugar we want now," said an acquaintance the other day as he picked up the sugar bowl and emptied the last of its contents of about 4 or 5 spoons of sugar into his coffee cup.

"We may have all the sugar we wish now—if we have the money to pay for it," remarked a friend to me as we sat at table together, a few days later. And he helped himself to 1 spoon of sugar for his coffee.

It is interesting to notice the difference in the way people are reacting from the strain and struggle of the war. Some evidently feel that since the war is over all restraints are removed and they are going back to their old, reckless ways of spending and waste. Others have thoroughly learned the lesson of carefulness and economy. "When I make over an old hat or dress and save buying new, I save something when prices are as high as they are now," I overheard one woman say to another, and I thought she was entirely right.

It is surely worth one's time to be careful of clothing now and to take the time to repair and make over. If we will think of how much we accomplished by being careful with food, we cannot help but realize that it pays to eliminate waste in that direction. There has been so much loss and suffering and cost in the war that we should carefully salvage from its wreck all the good that is in any way possible to bring out of it.

What we have learned of economy and frugality; of substituting for too rich dishes those which are plainer, really more palatable and much healthier; of a more simple though equally beautiful way of dressing, should be of great value to us personally and nationally—unless we

foolishly make haste to forget these lessons of the hard years just passed.

From a careful reading of the news from all over the world, it appears to me that the economy and thrift of the people of the nations will be of as much importance during the next few years as it has been during the actual warfare and may well determine in the end who are the actual victors in the conflict.

I notice that there is a systematic effort being made to buy up the bonds of small denominations from the small bond holders, and I am very sorry to learn that some are selling. I wish all might be like one farm woman of my acquaintance, who with her egg money has invested $350 in Liberty Bonds and who says she has formed the habit of buying bonds and will begin buying farm loan bonds as soon as there are no more Liberty Bonds for sale.

The Bettmann Archive

Liberty Bonds helped finance WWI.

Never before have government bonds of small denominations been placed within easy reach of the people of the United States. It

has given us all a chance to own a financial interest in our government and to pay interest to ourselves instead of to the other fellow, a way of evening things by making one hand wash the other, so to speak.

Some of us have been rather inclined, at times, to envy the government pensioners and to wish that we might be assured of a pension for our old age. Now here at last is our chance to earn our old age pension from the government by practicing economy now and remembering that government bonds, either Liberty Bonds at 4¼ per cent or farm loan bonds at 4½ per cent, are good, safe investments and worth making an effort to buy and to keep.

I am not urging that we become penurious or deny ourselves or our family the things we should have for our comfort and pleasure but simply that we never again fall into the way of thinking that we must buy anything because our neighbor has it or enter into the old strife for show. The reputation of a careless spender is nothing to be desired. For myself, I would prefer a government bond in a safety deposit.

Who'll Do the Women's Work?

April 5, 1919

Flaring headlines in the papers have announced that "women will fight to hold jobs," meaning the men's jobs which they took when the men went to war. What to do about the situation seems to be a very important question. One would think that there must have been a great number of women who were idle before the war. If not, one wonders what has become of the jobs they had. To paraphrase a more or less popular song—I wonder who's holding them now?

With men by the thousands out of work and the unemployment situation growing so acute as to cause grave fears of attempted revolution, women by the hundreds are further complicating affairs by adding their numbers to the ranks of labor, employed, unemployed, or striking as the case may be.

We heard nothing of numbers of women who could not find work before the war. They were all busy, apparently, and fairly well satisfied. Who is doing that work they left, to fill the places of men who went into the army, or is that work undone?

It would be interesting to know and it seems strange that while statistics are being prepared and investigations made of every subject under the sun, no one has compiled the records of "The Jobs Women Left or Woman's Work Undone."

But however curious we may be about the past, we are more vitally interested in the future. Will these women take up their old work and give the men a chance to go back to the places they will thus leave vacant? The women say not.

The Bettmann Archive

A woman's place is in the factory.

Other women, also, besides those who took men's jobs, have gone out of the places they filled in pre-war days, out into community and social work and government positions which were created by and because of the war. Will these women go back? And again we hear them answer, "Never! We never will go back!" All this is very well, but where are they going and with them all of us? I think this query could most truthfully be answered by a slang expression, which though perhaps not polished is very apt—"We don't know where we're going but we're on our way."

It makes our hearts thrill and our heads rise proudly to think that women were found capable and eager to do such important work in the crisis of war-time days. I think that never again will anyone have the courage

to say that women could not run world affairs if necessary. Also, it is true that when men or women have advanced they do not go back. History does not retrace its steps.

But this too is certain. We must advance logically, in order, and all together if the ground gained is to be held. If what has hitherto been woman's work, in the world, is simply left undone by them, there is no one else to take it up. If in their haste to do other, perhaps more showy things, their old and special work is neglected and only half done, there will be something seriously wrong with the world, for the commonplace, home work of women is the very foundation upon which everything else rests.

Never again will anyone have the courage to say that women could not run world affairs.

So if we wish to go more into world affairs, to have the time to work at public work, we must arrange our old duties in some way so that it will be possible. We cannot leave things at loose ends, no good housemother can do that, and we have been good housekeepers so long that we have the habit of finishing our work up neatly.

Women in towns and villages have an advantage over farm women in being able to co-operate more easily. There is talk now of community kitchens for them, from which hot meals may be sent out to the homes. They have of course the laundries and the bake shops already.

We farm women, at least farm mothers, have stayed on the job, our own job, during all the excitement. We could not be spared from it as we realized, so there is no question of our going back or not going back. We are still doing business at the old place, in kitchen and garden and poultry yard, and no one seems to be trying to take our job from us.

But we do not wish to be left too far behind our sisters in towns and cities. We are interested in social and world betterment; in religion and politics; we might even be glad to do some work as a sideline that would give us a change from the old routine. We would like to keep up, if any one can

keep up with these whirling times, and we must have more leisure from the treadmill if we are to do any of these things. We must arrange our work differently in some way. Why not a laundry for a farm neighborhood and a bakery also, so situated that they will be easily accessible to a group of farms? Perhaps if we study conditions of labor and the forward movements of the world as related to the farm, we may find some way of applying the best of them to our own use.

CHAPTER 10

Women of the 1920s: Articles by Laura Ingalls Wilder in the *Missouri Ruralist*

Small town life, as novelists Sinclair Lewis and Sherwood Anderson wrote, can be horrible, parochial, and stultifying; or, in the philosophy of a person like Laura Ingalls Wilder, it can be anything you want it to be, because you are the determining factor in what you make of your situation.

Mrs. Wilder saw that women in the 1920s, even on a farm, could choose the roads they traveled down. In "The Roads Women Travel," she writes about the parallels between roads and the choices women make.

For her column, "The Farm Home" in the *Missouri Ruralist* (February 5, 1916) she wrote: "We are told that the life of a woman on a farm is narrow and that the monotony of it drives many farm women insane. That life on a farm as elsewhere is just what we make it, that much and no more, is being proved every day by women who, like this one, pick up a thread connecting farm life with the whole, great outside world."

"Life . . . is just what we make it."

Mrs. Wilder was not one to let geographic location and vocation and the limits of her two terms of high school hold her back from the "threads" that connected her "with the whole, great outside world." One fortuitous thread was Laura's daughter, Rose, world traveler, Red Cross publicist, and bachelor girl.

Nobody worked harder than Mrs. Wilder to see that she wasn't left completely behind. She and Rose corresponded a great deal. She visited Rose to learn more about writing, and though she never attained the grammatical skills of her daughter, she never gave up on her goals of self-improvement and self-education. Mrs. Wilder was not an unlearned woman as some might conclude from her limited background; no, she was a self-educated woman. There is a tremendous difference. The fact is, the major impetus for Mrs. Wilder's development as a person and as a writer may have come through her club work, another thread connecting her with "the whole, great outside world."

Herbert Hoover Presidential Library

Mrs. Wilder always looked ahead and tried to make the best of everything.

Make that clubs, plural, as you shall see—one club, the Athenians, in particular. Mrs. Wilder was such a joiner and doer there never was enough time in her day. She complained frequently of the frenetic pace of everyday life in her many *Ruralist* columns. But such complaining did not stop her from joining more and more clubs or from promoting practically any civic and intellectual activity with zeal and enthusiasm. SH

The Roads Women Travel

February 1, 1921

Sometimes life presents us with too many choices. So it must have seemed to Laura Ingalls Wilder. In her youth, there was practically only one choice for women—whether to marry or not to marry. Often there wasn't even much choice as to whom to marry. A woman married the first person who asked her or she risked the "horror" of becoming an old maid, for that is what an unmarried woman in her twenties was often called.

By the early 1920s, that narrow tradition was melting away. Women joined the industrial work force during World War I, and the right to vote soon followed. With these new rights came expanded horizons and increased responsibilities—and new concerns. Would women be able to handle these changes?

Mrs. Wilder would have certainly answered yes. The road to new horizons must be ever upward and over stiff obstacles, but the view from the hilltop is worth it! SH

All day I have been thinking about roads. There are so many of them. There is the dim trail that leads down through the woods. It looks so fascinating, wandering away through the patches of shade and sunshine that I long to follow it, but I happen to know that it bogs down in the soft ground at the creek bank where the cattle gather to drink. If I go that way I will sink in the mud over my shoe tops.

If I turned back from the mud, it would be hard to retrace my steps,

for the way that is such an easy descent becomes, on the return, a toilsome climb.

Then there is the lane between the rail fences, a pleasant way also. Sumac and hazel grow on either side and there are wild flowers in the fence corners. It's safe but narrow, so narrow that persons cannot pass without getting out among the briars that mingle with the flowers at the roadside.

The main road to town is a broad, well-tended way. The roadbed is worked to an easy grade. Stumps and rocks have been removed, and the tracks are smoothed by the passing of many feet and rubber tires. But it is not pleasant, for dust lies thick along that road and all the trees have been cut away from it so that travelers become hot and dusty in the summer's sun and cold and dusty in the winter wind.

There is another road that I love best of all. It is a less traveled way to town, a quiet road across a little wooden bridge, beneath which the water of the small creek ripples over the stones, then on a little farther passing under the spreading branches of a hickory tree. From there it climbs the hill, rather steeply in places, I'll admit. But there are forest trees along the way and though the road is not very wide, still it is wide enough to pass, in a careful, friendly way, whomever one may meet. And when, after the effort of climbing, one reaches the hilltop, there is a view of forest and fields and farmsteads, and a wonderful skyscape for miles and miles, while on the slope at one's feet, the town is spread.

The view alone is well worth the effort required to overcome the obstacles on the way, and one arrives at the beautiful outlook without confusion or dust though perhaps a little weary and ready to rest.

From each of these roads there are other roads branching, some to the right, some to the left, leading into byways or toward other towns or back to some farmhouse among the hills. Some of them are full of ruts or of stumps

and stones, while others are just dim tracks into the timber or through the fields.

Roads have such an important part in our affairs! The visible roads are the pass-ways for most of the important events of our lives. Joy comes to us, light-footed, over them, and again our happiness goes swiftly down the road away from us. We follow them out into every field of usefulness and endeavor and at times creep back over them to a place of refuge.

All day I have been thinking of roads—there are so many of them—so many ways through life to choose from! Sometimes we take the path that leads into the bog with more or less mud clinging to our feet to make the toilsome ascent back, up the way that was so easy going down.

Sometimes we find ourselves in a way so narrow that it is impossible to meet others on a common ground, without being torn by brambles of misunderstanding and prejudice.

If we choose the way that "everybody does" we are smirched with their dust and confusion and imitate their mistakes. While the way to success (not necessarily a money success) and a broad, beautiful outlook on life more often than not leads over obstacles and up a stiff climb before we reach the hilltop.

Folks Are "Just Folks": Why Shouldn't Town and Country Women Work and Play Together?

May 5, 1916

Mrs. Wilder certainly followed her own advice. Newspaper accounts from the Hartville Democrat *and the* Wright County Republican *report that she was, variously, a member of a bridge club, Justamere Club, the W. M. D. A. (a short-lived state organization for rural women), the Eastern Star, and a charter member of the Athenians, who helped to found the county library. Mrs. Wilder had an incredible sense of civic responsibility and a need for self-improvement that impelled her to social activity.*

It is with obvious delight that she writes of her invitation to join the Athenians, for it seems that this club above all others met her need to be an ever more educated and useful citizen. SH

"The Athenians" is a woman's club just lately organized in Hartville for purposes of study and self-improvement. Hartville was already well supplied with social organizations. There was an embroidery club, also a whist club and the usual church aid societies and secret orders which count for so much in country towns. Still there were a few busy women who felt something lacking. They could not be satisfied altogether with social affairs. They wanted to cultivate their minds and increase their knowledge, so they organized the little study club and have laid out a year's course of study.

The membership of the club is limited to twenty. If one of the twenty drops out, then someone may be elected to take the vacant place. Two negative ballots exclude anyone from membership. There are no dues. "The Athenians" is, I think, a little unique for a town club, as the membership is open to town and country women alike and there are several country members. Well, why not? "The Colonel's lady and Judy O'Grady are sisters under the skin." (Mind I have not said whether Judy O'Grady is a town or country woman. She is just as likely, if not a little more likely, to be found in one place as the other.)

Surely the most vital subjects in which women are interested are the

Courtesy of Mrs. M. J. Huffman

Mrs. Wilder (center, seated) at a tea given in her honor by the Athenians

same in town and country, while the treasures of literature and the accumulated knowledge of the world are for all alike. Then why not study them together and learn to know each other better? Getting acquainted with folks makes things pleasanter all around. How can we like people if we do not know them? It does us good to be with people whose occupation and surroundings are different from ours. If their opinions differ from ours, it will broaden our minds to get their point of view and we will likely find that they are right in part at least, while it may be that a mutual understanding will lead to a modification of both opinions.

While busily at work one afternoon I heard the purr of a motor and going to the door to investigate, I was met by the smiling faces of Mr. and Mrs. Frink and Mr. and Mrs. Curtis of Hartville. Mrs. Curtis and Mrs. Frink have taken an active part in organizing "The Athenians," and they had come over to tell me of my election to membership in that club. What should be done when there is unexpected company and one is totally unprepared and besides must be at once hostess, cook, and maid?

The situation is always so easily handled in a story. The lovely hostess can perform all kinds of conjuring tricks with a cold bone and a bit of leftover vegetable, producing a delicious repast with no trouble whatever and never a smut on her beautiful gown. In real life it sometimes is different, and during the first of that pleasant afternoon my thoughts would stray to the cook's duties.

When the time came, however, it was very simple. While I made some biscuits, Mrs. Frink fried some home cured ham and fresh eggs, and Mrs. Curtis set the table. The Man of the Place opened a jar of preserves and we all had a jolly, country supper together before the Hartville people started on the drive home. It is such a pleasure to have many friends and to have them dropping in at unexpected times that I have decided when it lies between

friendships and feasting and something must be crowded out the feasting may go every time. . . .

Mrs. Wilder then goes on to portray typical activities of the club for her Ruralist *readers.* SH

At a recent meeting of "The Athenians" some very interesting papers prepared by the members were read. Quoting from the paper written by Mrs. George Hunter: "The first societies of women were religious and charitable. These were followed by patriotic societies and organizations of other kinds. At present there exists in the United States a great number of clubs for women which may be considered as falling under the general heads—educational, social, and practical. The clubs which may be classified as practical include charitable organizations, societies for civic improvement or for the furthering of schools, libraries, and such organizations as have for their object the securing, by legislation, of improved conditions for working women and children. In 1890 the General Federation of Woman's Clubs was formed. There were in the United States at the last enumeration more than 200,000 women belonging to clubs."

Get the number? Two hundred thousand! Quite a little army this. . . .

Mrs. Wilder finished her article by giving a taste of what sorts of papers and opinions might be expressed at Athenian meetings. SH

A very interesting paper and one that causes serious thought was that prepared by Mrs. Howe Steel on "The Vocation of Woman." "Woman," says Mrs. Steel, "has found out that, with education and freedom, pursuits of all kinds are open to her, and by following these pursuits she can preserve her

personal liberty, avoid the grave responsibilities, the almost inevitable sorrows and anxieties which belong to family life. She can choose her friends and change them. She can travel and gratify her tastes and satisfy her personal ambitions. The result is that she frequently is failing to discharge satisfactorily some of the most imperative demands the nation makes upon her. I think it was Longfellow who said: 'Homekeeping hearts are happiest.' Dr. Gilbert said, 'Through women alone can our faintest dreams become a reality. Woman is the creator of the future souls unborn. Though she may be cramped, enslaved, and hindered, though she may never be able to speak her ideal, or touch the work she longs to accomplish, yet in the prayer of her soul is the prophecy of her destiny.'

"Through women alone can our faintest dreams become a reality."

> Here's to women the source of all our bliss.
> There's a foretaste of Heaven in her kiss.
> From the queen upon her throne
> To the maiden in the dairy,
> They are all alike in this."

San Marino Is Small but Mighty

December 5, 1918

Laura wasn't overly concerned about contradictions and concerns arising from her increased freedom as a woman. She supported woman's suffrage and took great interest in her daughter's growing literary fame. After World War I, she frequently quoted her daughter's letters from Europe in her columns in the Ruralist. *It was around this period of time that the locals began referring to Rose as "famous," along with senators from the region and Yankee baseball pitcher Carl Mays.*

Clearly, Laura was proud of what her daughter was doing, but her own "liberation" still came mainly through the Athenians. We know of probably three pieces that ended up in her Ruralist *columns that were likely first done for the Athenians. The following one probably came out of a meeting on the theme of Italy, held on September 18 in Laura's own home.* SH

"In order to get my passport for Europe, I had to swear allegiance to the allies, including the King of Siam and the republic of San Marino. Of course I love 'em all if they are fighting for us, but it seemed rather queer to swear allegiance to that little four-by-nine country of San Marino," says a letter [from Rose] which I recently received.

Hidden away within the territory of Italy, completely surrounded by that country, is the smallest republic in the world. This little country, the republic of San Marino, is 9 miles long and contains 38 square miles.

The capital of the country is built upon a mountaintop which seems almost inaccessible, rising sheer from the plains of Romagna. There is a legend

that this mountain was raised by the Titans in their anger when they tried to reach Jove and drive him from the throne of Heaven.

The republic of San Marino has been free and independent for 1,600 years, while around it have rolled the strife and bloodshed of the wars of the world.

The position of the country, far enough from the coast to be secure from invasion by sea, distant from the great Roman roads, up and down which armies traveled, and the peaceful character of the country were partly responsible for it being unmolested, but the principal cause of San Marino's peaceful history is internal and exists in its institutions and the character of its people.

During all the years while other countries have been going through the disrupting, violent process of dethroning tyrants and vindicating the rights of the common people, there were in San Marino no factions, no tyrants, and the rights of the people were safe and respected. Here the people lived simply, changing their laws slowly as the changing times required and always adopting those changes which best developed and conserved their liberties.

It was in the middle of the fourth century, during the days when Christians were persecuted, that two stonemasons of Dalmatia, named Marino and Leo, crossed the Adriatic sea and came to Rimini to aid the Christian slaves who had been condemned to build the walls of that city. The lot of those who hewed the rocks from the mountains and transported them to the mouth of the river was much the hardest, and because their need of help was the greatest, Marino and Leo ascended the river and stopped before the two abruptly rising mountains. As they were experienced stonecutters, they were soon placed in charge of large numbers of slaves, whom they were able to help in many ways spiritually as well as physically.

When the walls of the city of Rimini were finished, the two stonecutters retired each to a mountaintop to live in peace and solitude. Marino hewed a bed from the rock and cultivated a little garden. The rock bed and site of the garden is still to be seen in the city. Some of the slaves escaped and followed their overseers to the mountains. A little Christian church was built on each mountain and here these simple people practiced their Christian faith undisturbed and the two colonies became an asylum for the weary and oppressed. Being poor and simple, their wants were provided for by the hewing and quarrying of stone, which is today the chief industry.

A wealthy Roman woman who had been taught the Christian faith by Marino, gave him the mountains which she owned as absolute and perpetual property. Marino strove to found a free society upon the foundation of liberty, justice, simplicity, charity, and love of peace, and when he died he called his people together around him and bequeathed them his mountain, "free from every other man." He begged his followers to be true to the faith and live in perfect accord as free men.

The territory of the country was extended a little through purchase and because of the warring times the city was fortified. The strong walls whose ruins still encircle the city show one reason why the little republic was left in peace.

The government of the country today still holds the spirit of its founder. A council of 60 citizens is the governing body. These councilors are elected every three years, and they choose from their number every six months two captains regent who hold the executive power and preside at meetings of the council.

There are several cooperative institutions in San Marino, among which are a public bake house, a bank, a canteen, and a grain magazine.

Fine livestock is raised by the people and every family has its own vineyard.

Actual criminals are not allowed to come and remain in the country but political refugees are given haven and many famous people have found refuge there.

Marino taught his people that war, though a necessity in self-defense, was otherwise an unpardonable crime, and so since its foundation until the present time, the country has never gone to war, but the people could not stay quietly at home while the war for the liberty of the world was raging, and the young men of San Marino went into the Italian army, and the country has maintained a hospital on the Italian front; for San Marino, though the smallest of the goodly company, is one of the allies.

One might well wonder after reading this piece from the early days of Mrs. Wilder's journalistic career if there wasn't more parallel development in the writing of Rose Wilder Lane and Laura Ingalls Wilder than has been admitted to. They both began to expand intellectually and journalistically at the same time.

True, the daughter's education was superior to the mother's, but it has been maintained recently that the only thing that "sings" in the mother's stories is the editing and rewriting of the daughter. Influences, however, do not all run one way.

It has been suggested that Rose, who, at the time the preceding piece was written, was a communist, did a sudden about-face after her trip through Europe following World War I, and then inserted considerable chunks of libertarian propaganda into her mother's stories as she edited them. But Mrs. Wilder's books weren't contorted into something by her daughter that Mrs. Wilder didn't already believe to be true—indeed, had

believed to be true all her life, both before and after her daughter's communist days. If anything, the daughter adopted the attitude of the mother, who proclaimed in 1918 that San Marino was small but mighty because its people had protected their "liberties." This ideal country was "free and independent," a phrase that occurs over and over again in Mrs. Wilder's books and is surely from her own writing and thinking.

Mrs. Wilder's other two pieces for the Athenians that later made it into written form were about the development of musical notation and the landscape of Shakespeare's rural homestead (which she no doubt learned of through daughter Rose). Yet even these seemingly unrelated topics show the mother's keen desire to learn and a fascination with scenery, which she would put to good use later.

The importance of the Athenian Club, then, can't be overlooked in Laura's development of thought and writing. Amateurs they may have been, but they were ambitious amateurs with a true genius in their midst.

Important also is this bit of historical memory from the club itself as to how Laura came to write her books. It is important to know, and it was repeated to club members over the years by the two members involved, that one day Mrs. Wilder called them, in strict secrecy, to come over to her place, for she needed advice about something. When the two members arrived, they found a big box of Mrs. Wilder's writings about Pa, Ma, Mary, Carrie, and Grace. Mrs. Wilder wanted their opinion as to what she should do with this writing, and both of them emphatically urged her to work on publishing these stories. These women always felt that Laura had taken their advice and that they were instrumental in the history of the series and its eventual publication. They told club members so, although their version of events never became a part of the official history of how Mrs. Wilder came to write the series in her middle sixties.

At an August 1950 tea held in her honor by the Athenians for thirty-five years of continuous membership, Mrs. Wilder expressed her delight in a little souvenir booklet made especially for the occasion. She left the members with the thought that as her life was ending she was facing a future that had no end. Finite would blend with infinite in the far beyond. SH

CHAPTER 11

Laura and Rose

Now Rose takes center stage—Rose, the famous and only daughter of Laura Ingalls Wilder. Rose and Laura began writing for publication at the same time, and neither had any trouble finding outlets for their work. But the parallel ends there. Rose received the far superior education in good writing. Her work for the *San Francisco Bulletin* was given the rigorous editing typical of those days when newspapers and periodicals reigned supreme and when reporters often regarded journalistic work as a prelude to a career in literature. Rose also wrote every day, another considerable advantage over her mother's efforts.

Rose authored two best-selling books in the 1930s: *Let the Hurricane Roar*, a book based on the pioneering of Charles and Caroline Ingalls in Minnesota, and *Free Land*, a fictional account of Laura and Almanzo's pioneering in South Dakota.

She made her living by her pen and corresponded with luminaries like Dorothy Thompson, famous columnist and one-time wife of Sinclair Lewis. To some students of the books written by Laura and her daughter, Rose was the only real writer in the family, with hundreds of articles, essays, and short stories to her credit.

Yet, in terms of popular reputation, by the late 1940s, Rose Wilder Lane became known more as the daughter of Laura Ingalls Wilder than as a celebrated novelist in her own right. Instead, Rose became more political and didactic as she devoted her time to the promotion of libertarianism through her books and essays. (To Rose, the greatest amount of personal freedom coupled with the greatest amount of self-sufficiency equaled a life true to American pioneer history and ideals.)

Thus, in her own eyes, Rose's magnum opus was a philosophical treatise, *The Discovery of Freedom*, a satisfying culmination of a personal journey that began in communism and ended with this rock-ribbed

South Dakota State Historical Society

Daughter Rose, the precocious child

avowal of the essential American virtues of freedom and independence.[1] This transformation did not enhance her hard-won popularity as a novelist.

While Rose was writing philosophy, Laura was credited with creating a fascinating personal account of America's history through the adventures of her memorable family. Her daughter's philosophical books, no matter how heartfelt, could not compete. Rose began to sink into something like literary oblivion.

This must have been a difficult turn of events for both women. It did not help much that Rose's presence in her hometown had worn thin too. Mansfield residents had become horrified when it seemed they turned up as characters in one of her books, *Old Home Town*. Townsfolk also found Rose outspoken, opinionated, and abrasive when women were still supposed to be more like Laura Ingalls Wilder: refined, pleasant, and soft-spoken.

Mrs. Wilder did the best she could with what must have been an increasingly awkward situation. She was always quick to say that her daughter was the real writer in the family. She rightly boasted of Rose's considerable accomplishments, as only she could know, for the evidence shows that Laura needed the editorial talents of her daughter as the series progressed. Their correspondence and the remaining manuscripts make this clear.[2]

Did Rose come to regret the editorial help she donated to her mother, which took time away from her own work, feeling that she was not getting due credit? If so, it appears that she never mentioned such feelings publicly.

---

[1]William T. Anderson, *Laura's Rose* (De Smet, S.D.: Laura Ingalls Wilder Memorial Society, 1976), 28ff.
[2]William T. Anderson, "The Literary Apprenticeship of Laura Ingalls Wilder," *South Dakota History* 13 (Winter 1983): 285ff.

Yet, the pendulum does need to swing back. Rose's skills as a writer and her generosity as a person should be recognized.

The truth is, Rose's greatest work was what she did for her mother. Something magic happened when they linked up as a team, because what started out as a simple set of stories of long ago ended up as a complex but unified saga of American family life.

Not all of the genius was on Rose's side. Mother and daughter worked together. *Let the Hurricane Roar* is, with fictional modification, approximately the same story as *On the Banks of Plum Creek*; and it is probably about the best writing Rose did on her own. It is good, but it is not a work of genius; *On the Banks of Plum Creek* is.[3]

Read them both. Weigh the evidence yourself. There is a mystery to the difference. One book lives, the other only aims at living. The words are all there, but the life is not. The Charles and Caroline of *Let the Hurricane Roar* seem like stick figures alongside the Charles and Caroline of *On the Banks of Plum Creek.*

Rose played a key part in the development of the series, but she was only a part of the equation. It's important that both mother and daughter get credit for the timeless appeal of Laura's stories.

Let's begin this chapter with an article that was published in the *Mansfield Mirror*, "Rose Wilder Lane Answers Some Questions about Women." Here you will see some of Rose's avant-garde ideas about women. SH

---

[3]Professor Rosa Ann Moore, then of the University of Tennessee-Chattanooga, developed a scholarly thesis with similar conclusions some twenty years ago. See "The Little House Books: Rose-Colored Classics," *Children's Literature* 7 (1978); 7–16; and "Laura Ingalls Wilder and Rose Wilder Lane: The Chemistry of Collaboration," *Children's Literature in Education* 11 (1980): 101–09.

Herbert Hoover Presidential Library

Rose, the high school graduate

Rose Wilder Lane Answers Some Questions About Women

AN ARTICLE IN THE MANSFIELD MIRROR
March 2, 1933

"We women know in our hearts, though we would not admit it, that men are not infallible."

Laura Ingalls Wilder believed in one kind of equality with men and Rose believed in another. Rose wrote this article at a time when her differences with her mother were most pronounced and in the open. Some people could not understand how two such different people could love each other so much and be so at odds at the same time.

Laura could say, with utter seriousness: "We women know in our hearts, though we would not admit it, that men are not infallible."

"Though we would not admit it" is a sentiment that shows such deference—from a woman like Laura who was so progressive—that even most of us men, from the most arrogant chauvinist on down, would smile at it. Rose differed from her mother in that she would have thrown such a sentiment out the window.

You can imagine, then, what sort of reception the following article had in the Mansfield community, which was far more in touch with Laura's values than with Rose's. This former communist, this world traveler, was used to a rough and tumble debate, in which she took the extreme position and stuck with it: "America was created primarily by women." SH

Rose Wilder Lane, Mansfield's best-known writer, and one of the best-known of present writers of the world, answers some questions of present interest to women.

"I am personally a pioneer," says Rose Wilder Lane, author of *Let the Hurricane Roar.* "As far back as my ancestry stretches, it's a long line of people going west."

Mrs. Lane was working for a San Francisco newspaper when the war dislodged her. For four years she did Red Cross publicity in London. After the war, she bought a house in Albania and settled down, but America was in her blood and she returned to her farm in the Ozarks. She is the author of *The Peaks of Shala, Hill Billy,* and with Frederick O'Brein *White Shadows on the South Seas. Let the Hurricane Roar,* published on February 21st, by Longmans, is a novel of pioneering in Dakota.

America was created primarily by women.

Do I find that life in America exacts any peculiar qualities of American women?

Of course. America was created primarily by women. The difference in character between the original colonies in North America and in South America was largely made by the fact that our colonists included women. If women hadn't done their share in attacking our wilderness, this country today would doubtless be inhabited by an entirely different racial mixture, which would have absorbed the Indian and the slave, as the South American races did.

Later, when Americans advanced through the mountains and crossed the Mississippi valley, the advance was a movement of farmers, and farming always depends on women. It is the one occupation that is impossible without women. And the reason the Mississippi valley is American today, instead of Spanish or French, is that the Spanish were adventurers and explorers, the French were explorers and traders, whereas the Americans were farmers who took and held and cultivated the land.

Even the feminist movement of the recent past in this country was

Rose, the liberated woman, on a walking tour in France

not women's revolt against oppression; it was a vigorous counter-attack against forces which threatened to push us out of our position as full partners in American life. The pioneer woman was as fully the pioneer as her husband. The farmer's wife always shares the work and the responsibility of managing the farm's business. When industrialism began to be more important than pioneering or farming, American women demanded their full share in industrialism, and that demand was the American feminist movement.

From the landing of the *Mayflower* to this moment, American women have always had a direct share in all American society. We can't take refuge in femininity at least without losing our self-respect. This country is our country; we helped to make it what it is, and we have to bear the results of mistakes in the past and contribute our full share to creating the future.

I don't mean that all Americans recognize this fact consciously, but it influences unconsciously all our activities and all our reactions to the circumstances of our lives. American women aren't "sheltered," either in good times or in bad; we don't expect to be. We are out in the world's weather, and a good many of us get pretty badly weather-beaten. We aren't remarkable at any time for feminine graces, but we are unique among the world's women for our development of human virtues.

It is said that the "fashion produces the woman." That is, that women respond to their own pictures of themselves, whether in their clothes or in their situations. Do you think that American women have changed through the various crises of their country, that the American woman can be counted on to produce the brand of courage the situation implies?

A great deal of nonsense is said about women. You have only to look around you to know that fashion doesn't produce the woman any more than it produces the man. (This frivolous-fashionable woman is a myth,

created in France during the reign of the Louis.) Modes of life vary in different times and different places, and women respond to the influences of their time just as men do. Of course we change; everything does. But if you mean to ask whether American women have abruptly severed all connections with their historical past, the answer is: Of course not; even American women can't do the impossible.

Certainly American women can be counted on to be courageous whenever courage is required. Some sixty million American women are answering that question right now. If you don't hear them, it is because they are answering it with acts, not words. They are taking the brunt of hard times today just as they always have in the past, and their fighting spirit is doing its share to pull us through. We are still acting in the tradition of the pioneer woman who fought behind the stockades when the Indians attacked, and of the pioneer farm-woman who worked in the fields and held the homestead against claim-jumpers, prairie-fires, crop-failures, and sickness and starvation.

Herbert Hoover Presidential Library

Rose, a "bachelor girl"

All our newspapers and magazines are full of the loud voices of men, wailing and warning and pointing with alarm. What are the women saying? Nothing. They're too busy to talk. Some of them are organizing and administering relief where relief is necessary, and most of them are thinking harder than they've thought for years, and all of them are somewhat pulling their children and

encouraging their husbands and keeping up their own good common-sense cheerfulness.

But don't you feel that they are too 'soft' for the hardships of homesteading, etc., since they complain so quickly over minor losses?

In my own little bit of this country, the Ozarks, hundreds of families without a penny are coming from the cities and trying to get a foothold on land that will feed them. Hundreds of one-room houses are made of logs or scraps of lumber, and you'll see the women helping to put on the roofs and shingle them. You'll see women working in the gardens and setting the hens and feeding young calves by hand. You'll even see them helping to saw down trees and chop wood to sell. They are doing their share and taking their half of the hardships, just as they have always done.

Two years ago the farmers in the lower Mississippi valley did something that years of argument and official pressure haven't been able to make them do; they diversified their crops. The women made them do it. The women canned so much food from their fields that they affected the whole canning industry of America. Try canning several hundred gallons of vegetables, fruits, and meat over a wood-stove in the heat of a Mississippi summer, if you think the women who are doing it are lacking in grit and endurance.

Of course the present crisis is producing the traditional courage in women. (And in men too.) The wails you hear on every hand are not the voice of this country. These are different times; there is a great deal of suffering, as there has always been when the processes of increasing prosperity in this country have changed their rate of speed. The same wails have accompanied the whole course of our history; every yelp of anguish and prophecy of disaster you hear today you might have heard in the early '70s

when Caroline was living through that winter in the dugout. You might have heard them again in 1893; I did. But then and now the mass of the people—half of whom are women—was silent and busy.

Our spokesmen are always just a little stupid. Neitzsche's loud trumpet-call, for instance—"Live dangerously!" Every woman knows it isn't possible to live otherwise than dangerously. Living is dangerous.

Do I feel that an aimlessness came with the passing of the 'old-time religion,' or was Caroline's courage part of the elemental nature of her fight?

It's a question of whether the old-time religion has passed. People cling to the symbols that have meaning for them. Bryan's fight for the conviction that the earth was created in 4009 B.C. wasn't a fight for that date; it was a fight for his belief in God. He couldn't believe that God created the earth by more leisurely geological methods, and he did believe in God, Creator of Heaven and earth, so he had to fight for a more literal interpretation of Genesis. Under the symbols are always the essentials of religious belief, and I doubt, for instance, that the passing of belief in hell-fire has really altered the quality or force of religion in this country.

But the symbols and even the essentials of religious belief vary from country to country and age to age while the fundamental struggle of human life against the lifeless universe is always and everywhere the same. I wasn't dealing with religious belief but with the more elemental struggle when I wrote about Caroline and Charles. And so, in fact, were the American pioneers when they went west.

The pioneers weren't psalm-singers or quarrelers about creeds; they believed in God; they kept their powder dry, and prayed later. Don't forget that a greater part of the pioneer advance was made by Quakers and by

Unitarians and Congregationalists, all of which dispensed as much as possible with religious creeds and forms. Courage isn't a matter of religion; it's a matter of character. And human courage has always been adequate to the demands made upon it. Our very existence today is proof of that.

Mother and Daughter

THE PERSONAL RECOLLECTIONS OF TOM CARNALL, ALVIE TURNER, AND MRS. FLOYD COOLEY

As for Rose's abrasive personality, that needs a correcting word too, a word that comes from some of the Mansfield young people she entertained and befriended as she was winding down her stay in her native region. All throughout her life, it seems that Rose struck many Mansfield people as being rough and uncultured while they regarded Mrs. Wilder as refined and polished. No doubt many will continue a quest for the correct literary assessment of Rose, but a balanced character assessment need not undergo such a debate; for as the following interviews show, Rose certainly did have her admirers too. And if adults were not always comfortable with this strong-willed woman, at least some others saw quite a different side to her personality. They remember her as the most fascinating person they ever met, and the Turner boys, John and Alvie, had much to be thankful for in Rose's friendship, as you will see. Let's begin with the memories of their good friend Tom Carnall. SH

TOM CARNALL

Tom Carnall is mayor of Sparta, Missouri, and was a close friend of the Turners. John and Alvie Turner were young boys who came to live with Rose shortly after their parents died. They were of high school age, and Mr. Carnall recalls quite a few afternoons and evenings spent at Rose's place. SH

My first association with any of these people who visited Rose or who lived at her home was in 1934. Two boys were living there named John and Al Turner. John could have been just barely fifteen and Al was about sixteen and I was about seventeen years old: freshman, sophomore, and junior in high school. The whole graduating class of 1936 had only thirteen students! The whole school, grades 1–12 may have had 250 students, in one two-story building.

John and Alvie came from Douglas County just south of Wright County. Their grandfather [uncle] was sheriff there, and they had one sister that I knew about. But their parents were dead, to my remembrance. My folks' property adjoined Rose's parents' property. She was living on the old home place but had built a place for Laura and Almanzo. According to my folks, the Wilders weren't real happy about living there but begrudgingly went along to please Rose. Now as soon as Rose left Mansfield, they moved back into their old house.

Anyway, I got to know the boys because I lived so close. We got acquainted as the school year began in '34, and I would go out to their home periodically. Well, almost each day we'd walk home for lunch out there to her house. Since we had an hour for lunch, we would walk out there three quarters of a mile.

Now, as I recall, Corinne Murray would take care of the lunch. She was Rose's housekeeper, companion, and driver, and Corinne worked out there almost all the time; but her husband worked in town. Corinne was a real good cook, and she did a real good job of taking care of Rose's property. That left Rose time for her work.

Periodically, Rose would just isolate herself and write. She would retire to the upstairs of this two-story home and begin working. She didn't want to be bothered when she was writing, so we knew to be quiet

whenever she was upstairs. Sometimes she might not come down for days on end; you wouldn't see her for maybe two or three weeks. I think her most famous book was *Let the Hurricane Roar*; and although I didn't read it, I know my father liked it.

Once in a while, when she knew we were there, she'd come down and say hi to us. Maybe she would get a cup of coffee and walk around a little bit, but then she'd go right back to work. I'd say she was a very even-tempered, good-natured old lady. That's how I saw her then, as an elderly lady. [Rose would have been in her late forties.]

Although she didn't eat with us, I do remember a comical incident about lunch. Rose and Corinne were gone that day, and we came in to get something to eat. We went to the refrigerator and found what we thought was a pretty good batch of minced ham. We made sandwiches right quick, drank a couple of glasses of milk, and went on back to school.

That evening, I went back with John and Al to play for a while before I went home. When we went inside, Corinne asked, "Did you boys eat that dog food that was in the refrigerator?"

"Dog food! No, we didn't eat any dog food. We had some of that minced ham."

"My goodness," she said, "that wasn't minced ham; that was dog food I put in there."

Those dog food sandwiches didn't bother us at all.

Rose started these parties to get John and Al better acquainted with the other kids in town. We are not talking about a large group of people, but it got to be a regular thing. She even had a dance pavilion built by a real good carpenter named Bruce Prock who lived just across the road on some old Wilder land that was bisected by Highway 60, which runs past the house.

My remembrance is that the dance pavilion was probably about thirty

feet square and was screened in, with glass windows so it could be closed up in the wintertime. It had a nice dance floor, good lights, and heating. There would be parties there about every Friday or Saturday night. If there was a ball game on Friday night, then the party was on Saturday. She was really interested in young people, and the parties were always chaperoned. They usually ran from about seven o'clock until about eleven; something like that.

We never learned how to dance much beyond some waltz steps. Let's see, I'm trying to think of some of the records we brought to play on the old victrola. Big bands were popular back then; I think it was the Dorsey brothers. Actually, we had a big radio, a console type of instrument that had a phonograph. I'd call it slow and easy music that we had to dance to.

The refreshments would typically be stuff like lemonade and popcorn. There was no alcohol, no smoking, nothing like that at that time. She didn't approve of that at all.

Sometimes it was just too cold to dance, and we'd come into the house and go to the west room where the big fireplace is. The kids would have popcorn and soda pop, and Rose would tell true stories from her life.

Now Rose was a master storyteller. She could absolutely enthrall you by the fascinating way she could describe a situation and get you right into it. One night I happened to turn around while she was talking and looked at the group. There must have been twenty of us. It was the first time I ever saw high school kids so interested in a thing that a lot of them had their mouths open like little kids of five and six years old. They were so enthralled by this story that they didn't even realize what their facial expressions were!

Generally, she told adventure stories. For example, she was a great lover of Albania and had been there, I think, shortly after World War I. She became really attached to the people and just fell in love with the country,

so many of her tales were about Albania and their striving for liberty. Now I understood that she may have gone back there shortly before World War II or even during World War II to help these people in their fight against Germany. Maybe she was even in the underground, but I never knew that to be true, for sure. It was just worded around. So far as I know, she never read any of her writings to us.

She was quite busy all of the time, but you never did know what she was writing. Eventually, she moved to Columbia to the Tiger Hotel, where she rented a rather large apartment. She was doing research, I believe, and Al went up there to go to the university.

In the spring of the year I graduated, 1936, she told me that if I wanted to go to college, and if I'd go work and make enough to pay my tuition, she would furnish me a place to stay up there. So that fall I stayed with Al and went to school one semester. That was all I got to go.

We didn't see much of Mr. and Mrs. Wilder. My stepfather worked with Almanzo doing repair work, fences and things like that. Almanzo was a rather small man. I'd say he was about 5′ 4″, best I can remember. And he had a club foot; it seems to me it was his left one. But he was not like the TV guy, the big strong man. At least not at that time, he wasn't.

Now Laura was the boss of the place, no question about that in anybody's mind. She ramrodded the whole thing. Yet she was very easy to get along with, congenial and all. But whenever she told Almanzo to do something, she meant it.

I had no idea she was writing too, but then she would have been communicating more with people like my mother, Violet Carnall. Seemingly, Mrs. Wilder didn't have a great lot of friends. They didn't associate with people in town a lot and didn't do much socializing.

I guess Almanzo was still doing a little farming. They ran some cattle

at that time and had a hired man to work for them, probably a pretty good number of cattle for an old Missouri farm.

Now Laura and my mother visited quite regularly, and I remember my mother telling me, after Laura began to write and sell books, that Mrs. Wilder had come over and visited with her one afternoon and wanted to know if my mother thought anybody would be interested in her life story, written for children. My mother encouraged her to write the book and said she thought it would be quite successful. Mother always felt good that she had encouraged Laura because of the success she did have.

I can remember only one time that Mr. and Mrs. Wilder ever came to any of our parties. They were over there visiting one evening when the kids started gathering in. I remember Rose saying to her mother, "Why don't you just stay and visit awhile. The kids will all be here soon, and we will have popcorn and sandwiches in a little bit."

"Oh, no, we don't want to bother anybody," they said.

"Oh, Momma, you won't bother anybody; the kids would like to see you anyway," Rose said.

That was the only time I ever remember them staying. They enjoyed it. I remember Almanzo sitting over there talking with some of the girls. He was stomping his foot in time to the music. I don't know whether Mrs. Wilder approved of that, but at least he was enjoying it.

I'll tell you a funny little story about Mr. and Mrs. Wilder and Rose.

There was a local boy who had a Model-A Ford Coupe, which he wrecked one night and tore up bad. They ended up taking the body off of it and making a stripped-down of it. John and Al wanted that thing pretty bad, so Rose bought it for them. She said, "You can leave it here on the farm. And, if you can get Tom to drive it, you can drive it to town once in a while; but you boys can't drive it until you are a little older."

Well, we drove it around all over that farm. Then, one day Laura and Almanzo came over to the house and were visiting. I was over there playing with John and Al when I heard Rose say, "Dad, what are you going to do; why did you come over?"

He said, "I need to go to the backside of the farm here and check a pond. I'm not sure there is any water in it for the cattle."

Rose said, "Well, how are you going to get back there?"

"Why, I'm going to walk through the woods."

"But my goodness, Dad, that's a long way!"

For a joke, I said, "Mr. Wilder, why, we'll just take you up there in this Ford we've got stripped down." But there was nothing to sit on except the gas tank.

So, we got him on that Ford, and we went up through the woods and down the other side; and he had more fun than a bushel of kids. He was just tickled to death. And Rose and Laura worried about him all the time he was gone till he got back. They were afraid we were going to tear the car up and him with it.

The last time I saw Rose was in 1943. She was still interested in John and Al, but she hadn't had any contact with them in quite a while. I told her what little I knew and that if I ever got to see Al I'd tell her.

Alvie Turner

Throughout her life Rose displayed an unusual generosity toward those in need. She seemed to believe that social security worked best when individuals met other individuals' needs. Rose had a way of "adopting" people, and when two boys living in the tough circumstances of the Depression came along, she didn't hesitate to keep them. SH

John and I came to be with Rose this way. Our folks had died about a year apart, so we were taken in by my uncle in Ava, Missouri. He was the sheriff, but he also ran the waterworks. He always carried two jobs; had to in those days to keep ahead with a family.

Well, John wasn't happy there—he was two years younger than me—he ran off. He would have been all of twelve or a little older I guess, and the next thing we heard of him was that some folks from Ava had seen him in Mansfield at a ball game.

Apparently, he stopped by Mrs. Lane's house one day and wanted to do some work for food, and she said she had plenty of work. She liked his work and fixed a place in the garage for him to sleep. After that she started him to high school. That's when people from Ava found out that my brother was up there.

Anyway, she felt that he needed to have somebody with him, so unbeknownst to me, she talked to my uncle about my going up there too. He said it would be fine with him, so he talked with me about it. Whatever I wanted to do would be okay, he said. He said that times were hard, and he didn't think he could put me through high school, at least not right then anyway.

My uncle said, "You can stay with me or go with her, but I think it would be better if you go with her because she'll put you through high school." So we both went to high school there in Mansfield. That was for three years.

It was fun living with Mrs. Lane. She supported us all the time in whatever we did. We did a lot of "experiments." If we were interested in electronics, she'd finance some of our little projects, tubes and things.

Of course, we did have chores. We did the yard work, milked the cow, checked the coal furnace, which was underneath the garage where today's

museum bookstore is now, and kept the hot water radiators going. The clinkers had to be cleaned out and taken away.

The other help on the place was Corinne Murray who lived there all the time and did the house-cleaning, the grocery buying, and the cooking. Her husband ran a laundry in town, but he stayed in town all the time. Once in a while he would be out for supper; very seldom though.

Mrs. Lane went to her typewriter just like a person goes to work, for long hours. But she never talked about what she was working on that I remember. I never remember hearing her or her mother talk about writing. Probably if I'd had my head up I might have, but I was only about sixteen or seventeen.

Mrs. Wilder was the prettiest old woman I ever saw. But the Wilders didn't get out much, not after dark anyway. Almanzo did chores around the house and kept the fences mended. We had one cow. I don't know if he ever milked the cow or not. We kept it across the road in a barn. We didn't have pets though; Rose was not a pet person.

I was never over at the Wilder place very much. If I had known then what I know now, I'd have spent a lot of time over there.

Really, Mrs. Lane became our family. It went great. She took care of whatever we needed. We bought our clothes from the Montgomery Ward catalog and went on trips to Joplin or Springfield in her Nash. Corinne did the driving and took us to ball games and the like.

Recently I read where Rose had been pinching pennies all that time. I didn't know anything about that. If we needed a shirt, we got a shirt. If she thought we needed anything, we got it. In the wintertime, she bought oranges. "Don't eat all this candy," she'd say. We'd eat all the oranges we could. She bought them by the case.

Mrs. Lane started the kids coming out. She wanted to do something,

so she started a French class, a one-hour lesson a week. Sometimes we would have twenty or so come out. She'd teach for an hour and then we'd dance for an hour.

You know, she spoke six languages. She must have picked them up just like that. She was fluent in Albanian, French, German, though not so good, and Italian and Greek. She was in Greece a good long while. She said one time that the king of Greece proposed to her; the king of Albania also proposed. But she didn't have any men in her life when I knew her.

Anyway, we danced for an hour, big band music of the day. Glenn Miller, Benny Goodman, all those guys. I believe there was some jitterbugging, but once in a while a friend would come up from Ava. He played the fiddle, and we would get together with him and try square-dancing. His dad taught him, and he was good.

I believe Mrs. Wilder and Mrs. Lane may have visited each other as often as three times a week, but this usually would be while we were at school. A lot of times Mrs. Lane would say, "I had tea with mother this afternoon." She didn't discuss her work; didn't discuss her mother's work.

Mrs. Lane was really something though. She could sure tell stories. We'd have regular meals if we weren't going anywhere. Then supper was a time when we'd sit and listen to her tell stories. She'd tell stories every night if we were there.

The stories could be about whatever you wanted.

"You want a scary story tonight?"

"Yeah," we'd say.

Or it might be a mystery story. She told a lot of stuff about her life as a story, a lot about her travels.

The place is pretty much today as I remember it back then, but the driveway looped in a circle by the kitchen door. And we got our water from

a well located about five feet from the back porch. She had an electric pump.

The furniture is pretty much as I remember it, but there wasn't the organ. I never saw her play a musical instrument. Jack and I fooled with the guitar.

Also the wood stove wasn't there either. That's been put there for looks. Mrs. Lane had a modern stove.

Our senior year Mrs. Lane moved her residence to the Tiger Hotel in Columbia, Missouri. That was about 1936, I think. I went up there to University High School and graduated. She sent John to the New Mexico Military Institute in Roswell, New Mexico. For a graduation present, she sent us both to Europe.

You see, I took a friend with me from high school—he financed his part. We hitchhiked up to Schenectady, New York, and John and his friend, a college student, rode the bus up there. Then from there we went on to Montreal, the four of us, and got on a boat. It was about $100 for each of us for the boat. I was in Europe for about three months, and it cost $300. Mrs. Lane paid all that.

After the trip to Europe, I tried college for a semester, but it didn't work out, so I went to work somewhere. We didn't write a lot; we sent Christmas cards and stuff like that. John stayed with her a long time, but I didn't keep in touch with him either. I don't write.

The most memorable thing about staying with Mrs. Lane was that we had fun. She had an outgoing personality, and she made it fun for us.

MRS. FLOYD COOLEY

Mrs. Floyd Cooley is one of the original charter members of the Laura Ingalls Wilder—Rose Wilder Lane Home and Museum and still lives in Mansfield. She remembers the dance pavilion as being something of a clubhouse, and the meetings were a very happy experience, there being little else to do in a small town. SH

Staying with Mrs. Lane was . . . fun.

We danced, you know. Al [Turner] was out here to the recent Wilder Day celebration and told about cranking up the old victrola. Now Jack [John] wasn't there. The last time I saw him was just after World War II when he happened to be driving through town in a red convertible. He saw my husband and I, and we visited for a long time.

I just know that we had a lot of fun when Rose moved into the old house. For a whole year we had parties out there. We didn't have any other place to go, and there was the clubhouse where we could dance the two-step, waltzing, some jitterbugging. I don't know that our dancing even had a name.

Before the clubhouse was built, I remember that Rose would read to us a lot. We would sit in the living room around the fireplace and listen.

The sorts of things we had to eat were things like cookies, oatmeal and sugar, but not chocolate chip. We probably had apple cider, and I do remember the gingerbread. It all makes for a nice memory.

Now I do remember times when Laura was there. I think that she and Almanzo were not happy in the new home their daughter had built for them. It was a rock house, and it has recently been purchased by the Home and Museum for restoration. But as soon as Rose moved back to New York or Connecticut, they moved back into their old place.

Mrs. Wilder was a very reserved person and never talked about her

books. She always wore a hat and gloves when she came to town; there was a feeling of sophistication about her. In the fifties, my husband and I had the Ben Franklin store, and she would come in and shop, and we would talk.

The sort of thing she might buy from the store would be something like flowers for the cemetery for Memorial Day. I know that one time she must have had someone else pick them up because she wrote us a note saying that just as soon as the weather cleared up, she would be in to pay for the flowers. She was friendly, not uppity at all.

The only thing I know about Almanzo came from my husband, who is deceased. I've heard my husband say that his folks' cow got over into Almanzo's strawberry patch, and they had to take him milk for a month to pay for it!

For the background on how Laura came to write her books, I would recommend *Laura's Rose* by William T. Anderson [available through the Museum's shop in Mansfield]. According to him, Rose had a lot to do with pushing her mother into writing.

CHAPTER 12

The Memory Be Green: A Potpourri of Reminiscences

When I first reflected on this project, I immediately thought, Surely the University of Missouri has made an oral history project of the Wilders and their neighbors in Mansfield. *After all, Laura's father was born in Cuba, New York, in 1836, well within his own elders' memory of the Revolution. What a fund of information such a project would provide on the beloved author whose personal history was practically a history of* America! *But that oral history was never done. We are left instead with a few jeweled fragments of memories with which to treasure the Wilders' past—and ours.*

And so throughout the 1960s and '70s and '80s, precious memory after precious memory slipped away as the possessors of these jewels died. They weren't famous people, but they were a precious resource of souls who knew the Wilders well and could have told us much about them. The memory of the Wilders was as fresh as yesterday's rain shower; there were no long ago and far away reflections to be attached to their neighbors up the road. I regret that we will never hear their recollections.

Yet all honor goes to those who have contributed to this volume. Though we will always wish we had more, we owe our thanks to them for what we've got. We are greatly enriched.

The following accounts were too short to stand as separate pieces, but when gathered together each one presents an aspect of Mrs. Wilder's distinctive character that confirms the uniqueness of her personality. SH

PEGGY AND ERMAN DENNIS

Peggy and Erman Dennis have been married over fifty years, and both were born in Mansfield. Though they lived in Kansas City for much of their lives, they returned to Mansfield in 1972 and have lived there ever since. Mrs.

Dennis served five years as chairwoman of the Laura Ingalls Wilder Day Festival held every year in Mansfield. SH

Peggy Dennis

I remember first seeing the Wilders as a child in town. My aunt worked for a banker's wife, and I remember that there was a costume party that the Wilders attended in colonial costume. That would have been around 1932.

My parents also ran the grocery store or supermarket in town, and the Wilders were regular customers. Mr. Wilder always wanted Mother to wait on them. He would come in, and she would sometimes playfully pretend she was ignoring him. He'd take his cane and rap on the counter. Then she would look up as though she hadn't known he was there.

They didn't know what had happened to his feet really; maybe it had been polio or something like that, but he had these heavy handmade wooden canes to correct the defect in his walk. He was like someone with club feet. The best I can remember is, both feet were affected, because at the museum they had shoes he had made for himself. Both shoes were made the same way with leather pulled over the toe and stitched.

Mrs. Wilder always dressed rather quaintly. Her dresses were always longer, and she wore long, bead necklaces. Her hair was white from the very first time I saw her. Mr. Wilder had a large mustache and was bald except for hair around the sides. He looked kind of stern, but he joked with people.

Mrs. Wilder was pleasant. She smiled a lot and, of course, was very interested in the library here that bore her name. She attended the open house for that.

Mother was also a cook at the local school. Mrs. Wilder was supposed to come on her birthday, and they were going to prepare her dinner. My

mother asked her: "What is your favorite thing? What would you like to have?"

Mrs. Wilder replied, "Chicken and dumplings."

First, she was going to come and eat the meal with the students. Then she was afraid that might make her nervous because she didn't like crowds, so she shared her meal with the ladies who worked in the cafeteria.

Another time, Mr. Wilder had been ill, and Neta Seal, who was a very dear friend of Mrs. Wilder, took Mother out to see them. Mother asked Mr. Wilder, "Is there anything I could fix for you, something you'd like to eat?"

"You would do that for me?" he said.

"I'd be glad to."

Herbert Hoover Presidential Library

Mrs. Wilder's unique dining room

So he asked for a double crust pineapple pie. Mother bought a can of crushed pineapple, made a thickened filling, sweetened it, and put it between two crusts. Mrs. Seal took it out, and he really liked it. A few days later, Mrs. Wilder came bearing a gift of candied fruit.

Coffee was 10 cents a pound. Bread was a nickel a loaf.

Mother's other connection with the Wilders is that she ran a little home laundry. For some reason Mrs. Wilder didn't wash the cloths that Mr. Wilder used to wash his hands and clean his goats before milking them. So, when he had a bag full, he'd come down and Mother would launder them. If Mrs. Wilder was shopping, sometimes he would go down to the house and sit on the front porch and visit with Dad.

From the time I knew the Wilders personally, they didn't farm much. Mrs. Wilder had chickens and sold eggs to people, probably the price was about 25 cents a dozen. How cheap things were!

I remember that at the Pennington market where we worked we sometimes felt the price of things was expensive. Coffee was 10 cents a pound. Sugar was like 25 or 30 cents for five pounds. Bread was a nickel a loaf.

Now I know for a long time it has been said that the Wilders built their own home, but the recollection in our family is that my husband's father, Ezra, and his nephew, Orel Dennis, built the original home, hand hewing the beams in the ceiling. They also built the kitchen, and it was considered quite modern at the time. It had a little open window from the kitchen to the dining room to pass food through. Water was piped down from a spring, and she was one of the few people to have running water so early. There are probably six or seven rooms to the house as completed with an upstairs and downstairs.

I might just mention that Laura wrote the words to a song called "Friends." Someone set the words to music, and a few weeks ago, some of us

went over to Branson, Missouri, and recorded it on tape. They will be selling it at the Museum.

Erman Dennis

Yes, my father built the house for the Wilders back in 1911 or 1912, although by hearsay, Mr. Wilder may have designed it. Then my father remodeled the kitchen in the late thirties and made it modern—for that time. Then he screened the back porch and took care of a lot of repairs through the years.

I really couldn't say whether the original house had a foundation although the house has one now. I do think my father probably had something to do with building the stone house that Rose had built. He was a carpenter and contractor and had something to do with practically everything built in Mansfield. [The Dennis family has lived in Mansfield for over 120 years.]

I do remember the Turner boys a little bit because they were at the home when father did some remodeling work. I graduated from high school in 1941, and they would have been there four or five years before that, but I don't know what became of them because my wife and I talked about that not long ago.

Personally, I would call the Wilders aloof people. My mother-in-law used to wash the old man's handkerchiefs he would use when he milked goats. I don't think the farm operation was ever really big. In fact, I think at one time they weren't making it on the farm and moved into town for a while before moving back to the farm again. They only lived about a mile from town, and a lot that they did was before my time.

MR. AND MRS. CARLETON KNIGHT

The Rev. and Mrs. Carleton Knight ministered at the Methodist Church in Mansfield from the middle 1940s through the early '50s. Mrs. Wilder was active in the Methodist Church throughout her years in Mansfield even though she came from a Congregationalist background. SH

Mrs. Wilder was such a sweet lady and gracious too. We'd go to her home, and she would fix tea and some kind of dessert, usually graham crackers with powdered sugar spread between them. We arrived there right after the war in 1945 or '46 and stayed for seven years.

Mrs. Wilder, who was around eighty, was just crazy about our thirteen-month-old son. She just loved him and wanted to give him things when we went out to visit. She gave him a pet. They always had stray dogs, but I [Mrs. Knight] didn't want them.

Mrs. Wilder always served hot tea; you'd almost think it was an English home. And she'd have a big apron on.

Usually, Almanzo skedaddled when we came. He'd be out sawing wood or something and didn't come in very often. He was shy of preachers evidently. We didn't visit with him as much as we did with her. She always came to church alone.

I [Mrs. Knight] don't remember the subjects of our conversation. One thing I do remember so much is that when she came to church, even in the summer, she nearly always wore a red velvet dress, a dark maroon red, with a lace collar. Her black shoes had a big old silver buckle on them. That was her Sunday outfit. Her hair was beautiful and white and done up in a knot on the back of her head.

By that time, she wasn't terribly active. I [Rev. Knight] never heard anyone say that she taught Sunday school, though she might have before we

came. My visiting was pastoral in nature, not counseling or anything like that. Almanzo didn't seem to be trying to deliberately avoid us; he simply always had something he was doing.

Mrs. Wilder seemed inclined to be pretty serious. She didn't "cut up" when we were around anyway, but then being around a minister tends to make people that way. What she did with the graham crackers was interesting because we didn't make an appointment with her or anything. As with all our church members, we'd just drop by. She felt she had to serve something so she'd stir up some powdered sugar, a little milk, a little cream, and put it between the crackers. She probably didn't bake a lot because her next door neighbor would bake bread for her.

I [Rev. Knight] don't remember much about when Almanzo died. If the size of the attendance [at Almanzo's funeral] had been above average, I would have remembered. It wasn't a large group, I'm sure.

Our church was pretty small. The membership was about one hundred, but forty or fifty would be at church. We also served churches at Hartville and Norwood.

I [Mrs. Knight] remember that we were at the library dedication. One of the neighbor women held our baby right over Mrs. Wilder's shoulder. Mrs. Wilder said, "This is important; I want the baby in the picture."

She didn't talk much about the past. Maybe she figured she had it all down in her books. She'd get letters from kids from Japan and all over and let our son have some of the stamps to play with. That was about all of the talking we ever did about her books; it had to do with all of the countries she had heard from. That's when we bought them for our son and read them ourselves.

DARRELL HUNTER

Mr. Hunter grew up in Mansfield and went into banking, spending forty-two years with the Hartville, Missouri, bank. In his retirement he still kept active in business affairs. Mr. Hunter passed away late in 1992. SH

He was very quiet. She did most of the talking.

My first recollection of Mrs. Wilder is of her endorsing royalty checks at the corner bank. I was working at a market store that sold furniture, groceries, and dry goods. The bank teller told me, "That's Mrs. Wilder. She's endorsing her royalty checks." That would have been around 1937.

I didn't meet her personally until later. I wasn't the delivery boy at the store, but I owned the pickup used for delivery. One evening she called down and wanted some groceries delivered to her home. Since it was almost closing time, I volunteered to make the delivery myself on the way home.

Mansfield Mirror, courtesy of State Historical Society of Missouri

Laura's writing desk

Well, I left the groceries, and she inquired as to who I was and all. I went in and sat down in the living room, and she sat down at the desk where she did her writing, and we just talked.

I can't remember what the subjects were. She probably asked me a bunch of questions. I enjoyed visiting with her. Her husband sat over there and didn't say much of anything. He was very quiet. She did most of the talking.

So, then I just made it a habit,

when she'd call down for groceries, to deliver them on my way home. I got even better acquainted with her when my wife joined the Athenian Club of which Mrs. Wilder was a member. That was a book review club that goes a long way back.

If I remember correctly, the tablets that she used in her writing were right there on her little desk. It was kind of a cheap tablet that you would take to school, like 50/50 tablets. If I remember correctly, she was writing in pencil.

Now I'll tell you something else. She had a daughter, Rose Wilder Lane. That goes way back to the early thirties. She had two boys, if I remember, I'm quite sure it was two. She lived in a cobblestone house on a road south of where Laura lived. It was set back quite a ways from the road, but you could see it.

Rose let the boys have a party, and I was invited. Several other people from Mansfield and Hartville were there, but I think that is the only time I met up with Rose. I don't remember where the boys came from, but I think she adopted them.

When I was still working at the bank in Hartville, I came across some old records from the Federal Land Bank Association. It appears in this book that Mrs. Wilder was the secretary, and the handwriting appears very similar to her writing. I wonder who would know about that?

I don't know. I just think people didn't really appreciate Mrs. Wilder like they should at the time. People get more popular after they die. When they started the television series, why, of course, that really put her on the map and her home.

DON BRAZEAL AND IMOGENE GREEN

Don Brazeal and Imogene Green are brother and sister. Don is retired and spends part of his time in Mansfield and part of his time caretaking a ranch near Branson, Missouri. Their father, Pete Brazeal, worked for the Wilders in the early 1920s. He earned a dollar a day. SH

"A dog named Ring . . . pretty much had the run of the place."

Don Brazeal

Well, I remember only one story really that my dad used to tell. He told us the Wilders had an Airedale, a dog named Ring that pretty much had the run of the place.

When Mrs. Wilder would come back from town with the groceries, she would give this dog the meat, which was fresh but wrapped in brown paper, and he would take it carefully in his mouth and trot off with it to the house. He would put it down inside without a tooth-mark ever going through that paper!

Imogene Green

Yes, Dad worked for the Wilders, plowing for him. And I remember about that dog. He was called Ring because he was black with a white ring around his neck. At noon, when Dad and Mr. Wilder would be working in the field, Mrs. Wilder would tie the message that it was "time to eat" to the dog's collar; and he would go out, right past my dad, and deliver the message to Mr. Wilder.

Another thing my dad always told about was that the dog always sat right at the table where there was a plate set for him. It was not a regular dining table but what we always called a cook table, and the dog ate with the rest of the family! You can still see that table at the Wilder home.

Dad said he could take a pair of Mrs. Wilder's shoes and hide them, and Ring wouldn't quit looking for them until he would find them.

My dad plowed for Mr. Wilder, and I was born back in '26, you know. Dad used their team of horses, so it would have been before when I was born that he worked for them.

Later, I remember Mrs. Wilder myself because I worked in town at the grocery store, and she would come to town every Wednesday. The store was on the corner, and I would see her go to the bank and then walk on down the street. I remember a couple of items of her dress: a little black hat and some high-top black shoes. She would be on her way to Daisy Freeman's where she always visited. She walked very straight.

I think she was friendly, but to just meet her she would be a "Good morning!" type of person. Not one to stop and talk.

FRANCIS GERVAISE THAYER

Mr. Thayer is the grandson of Eliza Jane Wilder Thayer, Almanzo's sister. His father, Wilder Thayer, was Eliza Jane's only child by her marriage to retired widower Thomas Thayer. Francis's grandmother is best remembered as the unfortunate teacher who got on the wrong side of Laura in Little Town on the Prairie. SH

I only can recall the Wilder place from one visit my folks made to the place in, was it '39? I'm pretty sure it was 1939.

My dad knew Rose real well, but she wasn't living there at that time. I only knew her by hearsay. I think Rose was considered something of a black sheep in the family, always traveling around and even into politics back then. But that is all hearsay. I think even J. Edgar Hoover had her on his mailing list.

We pretty much grew up with the Wilder and Lane books. My dad used to sit up and read *Let the Hurricane Roar* to us.

As I recall from our visit, Almanzo still had a few farm chores. It kind of sticks in my mind that he had some pigs, ten or twelve in a pen. Laura might have had some chicks.

Actually, we were just there for the day and spent the night there with them. Of course, Laura wanted us to stay on, but we couldn't because we were in somebody else's car. It was a friend's car and quite an adventure. We camped out, my older brother, my dad, and I. We had a big time.

Grandmother [Eliza Jane Wilder, Laura's sister-in-law] was treated pretty cruelly when her husband died. She was his third wife, and he had children by his other marriages. There was no real will ever written so the family took everything, her wedding dress, her wedding ring, because she was, they said, not part of the family. Everything he acquired after they got married was sold at auction. She came out on the wrong end of the stick.

But my grandmother was a strong one. She had homesteaded until one winter she was snowed out and had to give it up. She did anything to make a nickel. I think she sold Watkins products door to door. She was never at a loss; she always had something to do.

For some reason it sticks in my mind, maybe because it has been written about, but one of the main things I remember is that she was a good cook. She made fried green tomatoes.

ANONYMOUS

Mrs. Wilder once gave a talk to a Dakota school class. It made a lasting impression on one young girl who now, many years later, chooses to remain anonymous. SH

I can remember I was in the front row when she came to visit. It was a very small school, and I was in the fifth grade and very impressionable. I already knew I wanted to be a schoolteacher.

Mrs. Wilder came. She appeared to be a small sturdy woman, and she was dressed in dark clothing. I remember thinking that she was very old. She had a strong voice and a lot of poise, and I remember she held our class enraptured.

She talked about being a pioneer and what it was like. She had lost a child. She told us about that. But her emphasis was "don't be afraid of work or of overcoming obstacles; work hard."

There were only about twenty of us who heard her, but I had read the books in the public library just across from the school. I read her books over and over again.

One year I even taught in De Smet. They weren't doing much to remember Laura then, but my children have been there since, and I understand there is a Laura Ingalls Wilder pageant there every year now.

Part 4

Reflections

CHAPTER 13

Unsolved Mysteries: Sometimes the Question Is Who Knows What? Or, Does Anybody Know Anything?

Mark Twain once observed that as he grew older his memory became better and better until it was so finely honed he could remember things that never happened! But people who want to know about Laura Ingalls Wilder want to know what really happened.

That's the problem. We are all a bit like Mark Twain, and in a book of this nature, I have the additional problem of wanting the really "good" stories to be true so that I can use them. I want them to have really happened, but for one reason or other I am not sure.

So I have decided to present the following facts, suppositions, and queries. I hope that if some reader knows the answer to any of the following questions, I shall hear from him or her.

MYSTERY NUMBER ONE: Has Anyone Ever Found Laura's Cave?

This isn't a buried treasure story; but there are literally dozens of such stories from the Ozarks. They commence with the days of the Conquistadors and most relate how some Indian of the region passed on to an early settler the approximate location of Spanish treasure, which, of course, never has been found but presumably remains lost in one of the thousands of caverns speckling the entire region.

Laura's cave story comes about through a recollection of Aleene Kindel of Clarion, Pennsylvania. Aleene didn't know Mrs. Wilder personally, but she did do a lot of nursing home visitation in Springfield, Missouri. One day in her visitations she met a woman who had been in the hospital with Mrs. Wilder when Laura was very sick and toward the end of her life.

Mrs. Wilder shared with her roommate some of the experiences of her past and mentioned that early in her arrival in the Ozarks she and Almanzo and Rose had had to tough out part of a winter in a cave (perhaps the

unimproved log house on the Wilders' newly bought farm was not warm enough for the coldest days of the year?).

This story is all plausible enough, especially when you consider that Mrs. Wilder did spend part of her growing-up years underground, as she recounts in *On the Banks of Plum Creek*. The story does have a confusing element, however, because Aleene remembers her elderly friend as saying that the location of the cave was Pine Top (not on a map) near Hollister, Missouri (very definitely on the map but nowhere near where Mrs. Wilder is supposed to have ever lived).

I became inclined to discount the story until I talked with James V. Lichty, a grandson of Irene Lichty (see chapter seven, "Volunteer for Life"). Mr. Lichty had spent a summer at the Wilder home doing work for his grandmother. In the course of the summer, becoming acquainted with Wilder lore, he discovered that there is indeed a cave below the bluff of a hill, protected from the winds, which was part of the old Wilder property. It would have served nicely as winter protection. (The cave is not part of the homesite now and is not open to the public.) Aleene mentions that Mrs. Wilder supposedly did some of her cooking in the cave but that it was only a temporary shelter.

Naturally, confirming evidence on this story is hard to come by, but perhaps there is someone, still unknown to me, around Mansfield or Hartville who could confirm or disprove it.

MYSTERY NUMBER TWO: What Became of the Artifacts, or Where Is Mary's Organ?

There is a beautiful organ in the Rocky Ridge farmhouse of Almanzo and Laura Wilder, but it is not Mary's as was once claimed. Where, then, is

Mary's famous organ? It would seem impossible to lose or to destroy such an object, but it is surely lost.

Readers of the indispensable *Laura Ingalls Wilder Lore* newsletter know that the family possessions of the Ingallses were dispersed at the deaths of various family members. (Indeed, it is from the *Lore* that we learn that the organ at Rocky Ridge is not Mary's.) Small items that could be easily shipped were more likely to be saved than larger items that wouldn't be used.

Carrie Ingalls Swanzey, the last surviving Ingalls daughter to live in South Dakota, kept what she could, dispersed what she could, and sold the rest. When she herself died, in 1946, even more material was scattered.

The organ presently in the Wilder home in Mansfield is like the organ Mary might have used and has long been associated with the Wilder home. But its origin is something of a mystery. Mrs. Wilder herself did not play. "The only musical instrument I can play is the phonograph," she once wrote. Yet the current organ has been in the Wilder home for many years. Apparently, what keeps it from being the organ everyone wants it to be is the manufacture date and lack of any confirming evidence as to when it first appeared and from where.

"The only musical instrument I can play is the phonograph."

But Mary's organ is only one item. Almanzo had an entire shop of prized hand tools with which he made his canes, small wagons (recalled by Roscoe Jones in chapter eight, "Friends and Neighbors"), and furniture for the home. The fact that Mr. Wilder couldn't part with his tools kept him from selling the farm and moving into one of the Seals' apartments (see chapter five, "Friends and Travelers"). Apparently, the toolshed remained intact until Laura died and then . . . who knows? It would have been a wonderful display.

MYSTERY NUMBER THREE: Did Almanzo Spend Time in Jail?

Almanzo was certainly a law-abiding citizen. He may have been cautioned against driving his horses through town too fast, but he was well past horse-racing days when Mrs. Wilder penned a note to the back of an old photo from 1937 to the effect that Almanzo had just been let out of the jail!

The photo shows "the Man of the Place," seemingly without a care in the world, standing nonchalantly by some kind of wooden structure; and one is left wondering if the Wilders were having some sort of prank. I always wish I knew . . . "the rest of the story."

MYSTERY NUMBER FOUR: What Ever Became of the Gravity-Fed Water System?

When Mrs. Wilder wrote of its installation in 1916, their gravity-fed water supply to the house and barn was one of the wonders of the Ozarks. Water flowed from a spring down a hill 1400 feet to the house where the force of the water was such that it could throw a spray right over the home. They had their own fire hydrant! The cistern they constructed at the spring site extended three feet above the ground and was large enough to hold thirty barrels of water. The cement cover for the cistern took two men to lift, and the water was kept cool by the shade around the spring.

This wonderful contraption would seem to be too big to be lost, but it does not appear as though anybody of today's generation knows where the spring was or where the pipe was laid.

Of course, the house is on city water now, but even before it was, the Wilders had put in a pump that brought water up from the gorge that lies

close by the house so that by the 1930s the water was relatively close at hand. In any case, the old system is buried from view.

MYSTERY NUMBER FIVE: How Did Laura Really Come to Write Her Pioneer Saga?

With many famous events that become part of our recent history, some who have heard of an event also claim to have been there. So it is with just where, when, and how Mrs. Wilder decided to do her pioneer saga. Rose has generally been given credit for urging her mother to put her stories down on paper. Indeed, the evidence seems incontrovertible that Rose did as has been recorded.

But the evidence also seems incontrovertible that the idea of doing some writing of her own was Mrs. Wilder's from very early on. Indeed, Wilder scholar William T. Anderson has shown that Mrs. Wilder was working on children's stories, now "lost," by 1919.[1] And she was writing poetry for children at an even earlier date in the *San Francisco Bulletin*.[2]

Yet Mansfield residents remember just as clearly that Mrs. Wilder was discussing with them the possibility of writing about her childhood, with Rose being only a marginal factor in the beginning as Mrs. Wilder sought her neighbors' advice as to what she should do.

There are enough different versions of the beginnings of the series to make it clear that the idea did not come full-blown overnight to anyone. Perhaps it is the case, as in all good things, that how the good fortune came about is not as important as that circumstances all came together. Mrs. Wilder

[1] William T. Anderson, "The Literary Apprenticeship of Laura Ingalls Wilder," *South Dakota History* 13 (Winter 1983): 320.
[2] Ibid., 312.

and her publisher only foresaw one book, but public demand took care of the rest.

MYSTERY NUMBER SIX: Will *Pioneer Girl* Ever Be Published?

All but Mrs. Wilder's most informed fans would be surprised to learn that she completed a one-volume novel of her life that has never been published. The edited manuscript has lain unpublished for sixty years, and those who have visited the Mansfield home in recent years may have noticed several references to the "about-to-be published" *Pioneer Girl.* I remember that the notices were four and five years old when I visited the home several years ago now. But still no book.

Even if *Pioneer Girl* was not top quality writing (which it must not have been, for it was rejected by several publishers when first offered in the early 1930s), it would still attract considerable attention because of its autobiographical nature. Indeed, *Pioneer Girl* is reported to be the working outline for the entire series. The other factor that seems to keep it from being published is that it is very straightforward and factual.

Mrs. Wilder's fans realize that there are liberties in the stories. Apparently, *Pioneer Girl* would go a long way toward telling us how much and where.

MYSTERY NUMBER SEVEN: Shouldn't There Be a Thoroughly Complete Biography of Mrs. Wilder?

True, *Laura: The Life of Laura Ingalls Wilder,* by Donald Zochert and *Laura Ingalls Wilder: A Biography* by William Anderson fill some of the bill, but neither is completely satisfying. The Zochert biography is now dated, having been published in 1976 before many of the relevant papers and letters

became readily available. *Laura Ingalls Wilder*, published in 1992, is suggested reading for ages eight through twelve.

Mrs. Wilder will probably never be taken seriously as a significant literary figure (with her books acknowledged as seminal to the development of realistic portraits of children and their feelings in juvenile literature) until a serious biography accounts for her achievements. Even with her daughter's help, editing, support, and encouragement, Mrs. Wilder's stories are trailblazing in presenting life from the young person's point of view.

How refreshing it still is to read Mrs. Wilder's stories, and Laura's mind, when she tells of her vain sister and of her own jealous anger toward the one who had the prettiest hair! We feel as Laura feels when that pull, so strong in her father, makes her want to be moving ever westward away from old failures toward new beginnings. Whoever has read Mrs. Wilder has tasted some of the thrill of that attitude, has felt what life as a pioneer was like when everything seemed possible while the New World was still new.

None of her daughter's achievements and help should be used to belittle Mrs. Wilder's own life. Mrs. Wilder's history has never been fully recorded. Exciting aspects of her life in Kansas were left out because the incidents were thought to be inappropriate for children—they were.

Laura's Pa, Charles Philip Ingalls, turns out to have been even more of a distinctive character than the famous books reveal to us. Pa was several times appointed as "judge" when the family happened to be living close to civilization. Yet he saw nothing wrong when Uncle Hi took railroad property as "repayment" for what the Chicago and Northwestern had cheated him out of. To come out ahead in the Old West, sometimes shortcuts had to be taken.

Sisters Carrie and Grace each left written records of the family's early days that would enliven a Laura Ingalls Wilder biography. Carrie wrote

poetry and short stories and Grace wrote occasional pieces for the *De Smet News*. Even Mary wrote poetry, but none of this material has been gathered or added to a complete biography of Laura's life.

One thing that might emerge from a complete biography of Laura Ingalls Wilder is a more thorough picture of her husband, Almanzo James Wilder. "The Man of the Place," as Laura often referred to him, was a quiet man with more of an affinity for horses than people, yet letters reveal him to have been both a loving father and thoughtful husband.

Though physically frail, Almanzo developed Rocky Ridge Farm. He planted an apple orchard and worked the unpromising hill country into a 200-acre farm—no small achievement for a man whose first ten years of marriage had left the family poverty-stricken.

Yes, Laura Ingalls Wilder needs a major biography.

MYSTERY NUMBER EIGHT: How Did Laura and Rose Relate to Each Other?

This relationship has been touched upon earlier in chapter eleven, "Laura and Rose," but perhaps needs a further word here to balance the rather bleak picture presented by Dr. William Holtz in his biography of Rose titled *Ghost in the Little House*. Dr. Holtz unarguably shows that Rose's diaries reveal a daughter who both loved and at times almost loathed her mother. The question is, What do we make of it? Is there a side to Mrs. Wilder and the image we have of her from the series that needs to be concealed for the sake of her reputation?

No. Most of the really troubling years between mother and daughter seem to have taken place during the 1930s when they were working together. Laura was using significant amounts of Rose's expertise to get her children's books underway. At the same time, Rose was using much of her mother's life story to craft the book *Let the Hurricane Roar*, which would keep the family

South Dakota State Historical Society

Laura and Rose by a stream on the farm

farm afloat financially. (Rose had lost her money and her parents' money in the stock market crash.)

Rose did not tell her mother that she was writing *Let the Hurricane Roar*, which used Laura's mother and father as leading characters. Laura found out about it only after it had been accepted for publication and was horrified at the liberty her daughter had taken.[3]

On the other hand, Laura's extreme difficulty in organizing her own material made great demands on Rose's time so that Rose felt increasingly frustrated about being at her mother's beck and call. Does any of this sound fairly normal, or is it psychotic, as *Ghost in the Little House* implies? Many

[3]William T. Anderson, "Laura Ingalls Wilder and Rose Wilder Lane: The Continuing Collaboration," *South Dakota History* 16 (Summer 1986): 108ff.

relationships would be damaged by such a volatile mix of dependence and independence.

Laura and Rose were happiest when they communicated—at a distance. Their relationship definitely improved after Rose moved away and the Wilders could return to their own house, which Rose had taken over.

It is a testimony to the strength of family ties that mother and daughter came through their six or seven years of close proximity, collaborating and competing over the same material, with their relationship still intact.

Rather than assume the worst from Rose's diaries, we have to understand that throughout much of the terrible 1930s she suffered periodic bouts of severe depression. These episodes drained her, darkened her vision of everything and everybody, and left her incapable of work for days on end. "Worried sick" would be an apt description of her state of mind.

Rose pulled through this dark period to find something like peace and security in her latter days. As her fortunes and those of her mother improved so did their relationship.

MYSTERY NUMBER NINE: Did the Books Make Laura Rich?

Call it childish interest that we should want to know such things, but we do naturally wonder if Mrs. Wilder ended her days well off. And if well off, how well off?

We do have a few clues.

When Mrs. Wilder died, the Mansfield newspaper speculated that Mrs. Wilder was receiving something like $18,000 a year. If that is an accurate estimate, then that number multiplied by four to allow for inflation would bring her yearly earnings to something like $72,000 by today's standards.

This figure is all the more remarkable if her publishers held her to her 1930s contracts, which specified that both *Farmer Boy* and *Little House on the Prairie* earn only a straight five percent of retail, rather than the ten percent they gave her for *Little House in the Big Woods.*

Yet Laura could have gone back after the Depression was over and requested a better deal. Her agent, George Bye, could have pointed out, justly, that business conditions had improved and that Laura deserved a higher rate on *Farmer Boy* and *Little House on the Prairie.*

All of Laura's books continued to sell fantastically well throughout this period with very little promotional help from her publisher. In fact, the books sold so well in original hardcover that it was not until the middle 1950s that the publisher decided to issue a paperback edition, with the famous Garth Williams illustrations. Williams's illustrations took ten years to complete and were so hugely successful they nearly eclipsed the great work he had done on earlier children's books. Indeed, his illustrations are the only illustrations most people associate with the books.

Certainly, by the time Mrs. Wilder died, by Ozark standards she was a wealthy lady. For tax purposes her estate was valued at some $80,000, or over $300,000 by today's standards. She had some $10,000 in a bank account, an amount that would be high even by today's inflated standards.

Yet it must be admitted that this increasingly well-off lady probably never saw herself as being delivered from the economic wilderness of her early and even mature years. The Wilders never really had money of their own to spare until the early 1940s when the accumulation of their royalties became significant. "The Man of the Place" lived his entire adult life trying to wrest a living from the land: first in cruelly dry South Dakota, then in cruelly rocky Missouri hill country.

By then, the habits of life-long penury lay on them both. After Mr.

Wilder died, Laura closed off several rooms of the house. She lived mostly in the kitchen, the dining room, and her bedroom. The outside of the old farm home that had once been a showplace of the Ozarks took on a neglected look—drainspouts askew, paint peeling.

Laura, who relished the years of her early travels, spent the last years of life close to home, contenting herself now and then with a chauffeured drive through her Ozark hills.

MYSTERY NUMBER TEN: How Many Copies of Mrs. Wilder's Books Have Been Sold?

For years Harper & Row Publishers, the original issuers of the complete Wilder works, chose to remain silent on the sales figures of the books. While Agatha Christie's publishers would ballyhoo the latest ten million sales of the mystery writer's works, Harper felt no similar need to boast of Laura Ingalls Wilder. My simple 1990 request for an estimate of Mrs. Wilder's worldwide sales seemed to leave HarperCollins, the current publishers, sincerely dubious.

My request passed through the hands of so many functionaries, you would have thought I had asked for a private viewing of the Crown Jewels! In the end, the company provided no answers.

However, the settlement of Rose Wilder Lane's will did bring forth an accounting of some million copies sold by the end of the sixties (Mrs. Lane died in 1968). These are impressive sales figures but nothing like the sales figures that resulted from the production of the widely admired television series. Though some feel that this series trivialized Mrs. Wilder and her life, the fact is, book sales soared on its account. Paperback volumes were issued that identified the books more closely with the television series, and virtually

all editions of the books enjoyed successes far exceeding anything before the TV series.

Worldwide sales also soared because the Michael Landon series became one of America's best entertainment exports. People who had never heard of the books saw the series and then demanded the original works. Both the TV series and the books became special favorites of the Japanese.

In our past is our beginning.

Finally, early in 1993 HarperCollins decided to release sales figures on Mrs. Wilder's books in conjunction with its new series of children's books featuring the life of Rose Wilder Lane. Promotional copy for the Rocky Ridge series finally announced that some 60 million of Laura's books had been sold across the world. Not bad for someone who waited until the age of sixty-five before beginning to put her life on paper.

MYSTERY NUMBER ELEVEN: Why Has There Never Been a Realistic Film Portrayal of Laura and Her Family?

Ever since I first saw the stunning Anne of Green Gables series made by Canadian filmmaker Ken Sullivan, I have been disappointed that something equally attractive and authentic has not been done for the pioneer life of Laura Ingalls Wilder. There is fully as much story to the history of Laura Elizabeth Ingalls as there ever was to the fictional life of Anne Shirley, which was brought to life by television's "Wonderworks" program. American film simply hasn't done anything quite like it.

A truly good film about the growing-up years of Laura Elizabeth Ingalls would tell us more about our own American history than a thousand textbooks. And this is needed, for we have forgotten our common history, the shared beliefs that for the most part molded what was good about our country.

As we come to the close of the twentieth century, we need to reaffirm the values of hopefulness and optimism that used to imbue this country with a spirit of greatness. Life was not easy or simple in those days of long ago, yet our history, viewed through Laura's eyes, might clear our modern-day myopia about who we are and where we've come from.

In our past is our beginning. SH

Appendices

APPENDIX 1

The *De Smet News* Remembers the Ingalls Family

A remembrance of Mrs. Wilder wouldn't be complete without the story of De Smet, the setting for five of the books; the Ingalls family members were acknowledged to be the town's first citizens even before Mrs. Wilder became a famous writer.

And if you have carefully read Laura's stories, you will meet, through these following pages of the De Smet News, *some of the assembled cast of characters that made up Laura's real-life stories. You will certainly learn that the long winter of 1880–81 really happened, and the experience of that winter so marked the town's memory that the fiftieth anniversary of the town's founding has more than just a few references to those who lived through it. It was a badge of distinction to have participated in the struggle to wrest a living from the dry Dakota plains, as I mentioned in part two of this book.*

That's what the De Smet News *was saying back in 1930 when these remembrances were penned. Let the old settlers themselves tell you what it was like and what part the Ingallses played in it. You see, at least to some people, Charles Ingalls and his family were famous even before Laura memorialized them. Here is the town of yesteryear, the real "Little Town on the Prairie." As its people tell their story (articles appear as written, blemishes and all) familiar characters will come into view. Thanks to old settler Laura Ingalls Wilder, you will have met them before in her books.* SH

June 6, 1930

INGALLS WAS FIRST RESIDENT IN DE SMET
FAMILY OF R. R. TIMEKEEPER LIVED AT SILVER LAKE IN 1879; MOVED TO TOWN

A railroad timekeeper and clerk came to be the first resident of De Smet, and remained to take an active part in its development, he and his family making it their home through the remainder of the lives of the parents. This man was C. P. Ingalls.

In giving credit to those who took part in the pioneering of Kingsbury county and De Smet, Mr. Ingalls has the honor of being the first in several distinctions. He was the first resident, first to have a family with him here, quite possibly first to establish a home on the townsite, first justice of the peace and first town clerk.

Mr. and Mrs. Ingalls and their family drove from Tracy, Minnesota, the end of the railroad, to where Brookings is now located, the husband and father being engaged as bookkeeper and timekeeper at the construction camp. This was early in 1879, and in the late summer, as construction moved west, they drove from Brookings to the camp on the banks of Silver Lake, then a pretty little body of water and the resting place for all kinds of wild water birds—ducks, swans, geese, and pelicans.

In the Ingalls family there were: Mary, who died two years ago, Laura (Mrs. Manley Wilder), Mansfield, Mo., Grace (Mrs. Nate Dow), of Manchester, and Carrie (Mrs. D. N. Swanzey of Keystone).

Mrs. Swanzey recalls that the camp was a busy place, with many drivers and teams who returned to camp at night with clouds of dust, shouts

of drivers and galloping horses. That was the signal for the children to run in for supper and bed. Meanwhile the men showed rivalry over their teams and their knowledge of how to handle a scraper. There were some good horses in that camp and Mrs. Swanzey says it is no wonder that occasionally a thief would pick out a good horse, and when there had been visitors about during the day the men would sleep by their horses that night.

In the fall the camp broke up, the surveyors and graders went back East, and the Ingalls family moved into the cabin that the engineers had built, Mr. Ingalls to spend the winter looking after things for the railroad company. They bought the food supply left at the company camp, this including some hardtack.

The winter of 1879–80 was a very mild one, and Mrs. Wilder, writing from Mansfield, Missouri, to tell of those early days, reports that about Christmas time Mr. and Mrs. R. A. Boast arrived and lived in a little house within a few steps of the Ingalls. It was in that house that the Boasts entertained "the whole of De Smet and Lake Preston" on New Year's Day.

The two towns—neither of them yet in existence—were represented on that day by the Ingalls family and a bachelor named Walter Ogden, who lived near the site of Lake Preston. Mr. Boast always described the day as a warm one—so mild that the doors were left open.

The Ingalls home was a stopping place for the early home-seekers, and they played host as best they could, their house being practically a hotel that first year. It was also the scene of the first religious service and the family played an important part in the early religious history of the community described in another article in this paper.

Mrs. Swanzey describes the bird life of that first spring as the children recall it: "As it got warmer the wild ducks and geese began to come. Early one

morning there was such a noise that we ran out of doors, to find the lake covered with wild geese, swimming and splashing—every goose talking. Our parents told us that they were choosing their mates, as it was St. Valentine's Day. Mornings we would watch the lake, and with the wind blowing the water in little waves and with wild ducks and geese and occasionally swans, it was a sight no child could forget."

Mrs. Swanzey continues: "Spring came, and with it the surveyors. Father used to go with them and one day he came home and said the town was all located. After dinner I went to the top of the hill, east of where the court house now is, to see the town, and all I saw was a lot of stakes in the ground. I went back and told Mother there was nothing but a lot of sticks stuck in the ground and she told me that where they were would be houses, stores, a schoolhouse and a church."

Relieved of his railroad caretaker job Mr. Ingalls moved to town, building a small place where the Penny store now is, later selling it to E. H. Couse for a hardware store. He then built a small place diagonally across the corner and there the family lived. Mr. Ingalls was one of the first justices of the peace of the county and the first justice court was held in the front room of this small house. Church services were held there, too.

[Editor's note: From the official minutes of 1880, we read that E. W. Smith was appointed justice in April but moved away in May, and Mr. Ingalls succeeded him.]

In her letter about the early history Mrs. Wilder tells of her husband's location on his homestead in 1879, but states that he went back to "civilization" for the winter and they did not meet until some time later. He spent the winter of 1880–81 in De Smet, as did the Ingalls family.

Mrs. Swanzey closes her letter: "Details slip my memory but

impressions last, and the lives of the early pioneers were bound together in an effort to build for the future, not only a town but a good town. There are others who can tell you better of the Hard Winter, of grinding wheat in coffee mills for flour, of the snow and drifts and the spirit of comradeship in the little town."

The Ingalls family were to move later to their farm southeast of town and live there some years. Later they lived in De Smet on Third street, both parents passing away here.

June 6, 1930

DE SMET'S PIONEER CHURCH IS CELEBRATING FIFTIETH ANNIVERSARY THIS YEAR, TOO

Laura's favorite minister of her youth, the Rev. E. H. Alden, is mentioned in this recounting of the church the Ingallses helped to found. The Rev. Edward Brown, her most unfavorite minister, is also mentioned. SH

Churches played an early part in the development of Kingsbury county and of De Smet vicinity, this year of 1930 being the fiftieth anniversary of the organization of the first church at the county seat.

The church record [sic] of the earliest days seem to be lost. Notes left by Mrs. C. P. Ingalls, first residents, have been valuable to the church clerk, who has prepared this history.

The first church was named The First Congregational Church of De Smet, and the organization came fifty years ago this month, June 20, 1880. The Rev. E. H. Alden, working under the Rev. Stewart Sheldon,

Congregational missionary superintendent for Dakota Territory, held this meeting. Mr. Alden was given a commission to supply this field for the first six months of 1880. Among those present at this first service were Mr. and Mrs. C. P. Ingalls, Mary, Laura, Carrie and Grace, Mr. and Mrs. R. A. Boast, T. H. Ruth, A. W. Ogden, Mr. O'Connell and William O'Connell, and others, making twenty-five in all.

The missionary went on west but returned for later services, held in this house until May, when the depot was partly completed and they were held there, the agent, Rev. H. G. Woodworth, holding them part of the time.

In May, Mr. Alden relinquished the field to the Rev. Edward Brown, and it was he who on June 20, 1880, at a meeting in the still unfinished depot, organized the First Congregational Church of De Smet. The membership was Mr. and Mrs. C. P. Ingalls and Mary, the Rev. and Mrs. Edward Brown, Mr. and Mrs. S. N. Gilbert and V. V. Barnes, all joining by letter from other churches. Mr. Barnes was chosen as clerk.

The next record Mr. Mallery finds is of the October sixth meeting, when the articles of incorporation were drawn and signed by Mr. Barnes, Mr. Brown, S. C. Sherwin, C. L. Ingalls [Caroline Lake Ingalls, Mrs. Ingalls], Orville Sherwin, Mary Ingalls and C. P. Ingalls. Under this organization a regular meeting was held at three p.m., October 9, 1880, at the home of Mr. Barnes, and he, Mr. Ingalls and S. N. Gilbert were elected trustees. The articles of incorporation were sent to Yankton and filed, and on November 10, 1880, a Certificate of Corporate Existence was granted to the church by the secretary of the territory. . . .

June 6, 1930

RICHARDSON NEAR DE SMET FOR HARD WINTER

According to this report, the year of the hard winter provided a clear Christmas Day on which seventy-five people celebrated the season at the Ingallses'! SH

In February, 1880, R. H. Richardson with his brother, E. A. Richardson, and Wm. H. Hare answered to the call of the West, coming from New Lisbon, Wisconsin, to file on homesteads in the vicinity of Erwin. The C. & N. W. railroad came only as far as Volga then and they were obliged to travel by team from there.

Each built a small frame house, the lumber being hauled from Volga. The houses were sodded to the eaves. They then proceeded to plow land and plant a crop of rutabagas, also a few potatoes. The crops were wonderfully fine but an early blizzard in October took all of the potatoes, though they were able to harvest the rutabagas.

Mr. Hare's family came in the spring of 1880 but Mr. Richardson's wife and daughter and E. A. Richardson's family came in November of that year.

For fuel they burned twisted hay. The Richardson brothers each had a yoke of oxen, a cow and one horse between them.

The fall and early winter was fine and Christmas Day people from far and wide gathered at the Ingalls home for a picnic dinner. There were about seventy-five persons present; most of them were strangers, however, they quickly became acquainted and all had a happy time. During that day the snow began falling and from then until the next May it was mostly blizzards and blockades. Provisions became scarce. The Richardsons had brought

enough flour to last through the winter but when the neighbors became low on provisions they loaned to them until they had none left and then were obliged to grind wheat in a small coffee mill for bread. The bread was made without yeast or milk or butter—just stirred up with a little water and vinegar and baked. It was exceedingly healthful. The rutabagas served for potatoes and desserts, eating them either cooked or raw and they were quite delicious. Coffee, tea and sugar were things to dream of.

The Richardson's little coffee mill and sieve went the rounds, supplying four or five families with flour. Wheat was bought from Amos Whiting and hauled a distance of five miles on hand sleds over the frozen drifts, the snow being too deep for oxen to travel. By the time spring came these people were indeed hungry for something good to eat. . . .

APPENDIX 2

Reflections in the *Mansfield Mirror*, the *Hartville Democrat*, the *Wright County Republican*, and the Mansfield Centennial Album

The following fragments and complete articles focus on Laura Ingalls Wilder as seen through the eyes of the Wright County, Missouri, community. These local views show how Mrs. Wilder's presence and influence became a major part of her neighbors' lives.

The articles chronicle the progress of her life from active club woman and local celebrity to nationally recognized author. All along, different members of her community take note of Mrs. Wilder's life and career and comment on what she meant to them and to her home town.

Each article is presented here as it first appeared.

The Wright County Republican *of November 17, 1911, begins one of the earliest chronicles of Mrs. Wilder's civic and publishing activities. All of this and farm wife too!* SH

MRS. A. J. WILDER

Several farmers, and particularly those interested in poultry, have inquired who Mrs. A. J. Wilder is. This question was asked again by Rev. David Long, who lives in the eastern portion of the county and who in company with several gentlemen called on the *Republican* last week. Mrs. A. J. Wilder and her husband reside on Rocky Ridge Farm, one mile east of Mansfield. Mrs. Wilder has for some years been a contributor to various state publications. At present she is editor of the poultry department of the *Star Farmer.* She also contributes to the *Missouri Ruralist* and is on the Staff of the *Globe Democrat,* as well as several eastern papers. A visit to Rocky Ridge Farm would probably give the inquirer a better insight to poultry raising than what could be obtained in any other section of South Missouri.

Two newspaper references from the Hartville Democrat *(June 22, 1916 and September 26, 1918) indicate that Mrs. Wilder didn't feel the least bit uncomfortable about entertaining one of the numerous clubs of which she was a member. Her home had become one of the showplace farm houses of the Ozarks.* SH

ATHENIAN CLUB

The members of the Athenian Club met at one o' clock in the courtyard on Thursday afternoon and were taken in autos to the beautiful home of Mrs. A. J. Wilder one mile east of Mansfield, where one of the most pleasant meetings of the club was held. The meeting was called to order by the President Mrs. A. M. Curtis. Mrs. D. D. Killam was leader of the meeting. Each member present responded to the roll call by giving the name of a late novel and its author. The subject of the lesson, "Novels of Today" was very interesting and instructive. The following program was rendered.

Paper—Literati of the Ozarks—Mrs. H. E. Frink.
What was Samuel Clemens de plume [sic]? What style of writing did he adopt? Mrs. Geo. Murrell.
In your opinion, who is the leading Novelist of today? Mrs. W. A. Newton.
What do you think of Opie Read's novels? Are his characters true to life? What of his descriptions of nature? Mrs. Dr. Wilson.

Reading—Mrs. A. M. Curtis.

What quality in Mrs. Delands novels appeal [sic] so strongly to the public? Mrs. A. J. Wilder.

Name Harold Bell Wright's best books and tell why you think them superior to his other works—Mrs. Geo. Hunter.

Discuss the "Call of the Wild" by Jack London—Miss Audrey Jackson.

Review "The Story of Art Smith" by Rose Wilder Lane—Mrs. A. M. Curtis.

What do you think of Booth Tarkington's Penrod?—Mrs. Howe Steele.

Discuss the merit of Gene Stratton Porter's writings—Mrs. Bert Ellis.

Compare "The Shepherd of the Hills" and "Gene Carroll"—Mrs. Ralph Simmons.

How is novel reading helpful and harmful? Mrs. D. D. Killam.

Music—Mrs. W. A. Newton.

Several books were named which have been written by authors from the Ozarks and who are still doing good work along this line.

During the social half hour the hostess, assisted by Mrs. N. J. Craig of Mansfield, served dainty refreshments to the club. . . .

ATHENIANS MEET AT THE WILDER HOME NEAR MANSFIELD

The Athenian Club met on Wednesday afternoon September 18th at the beautiful home of Mr. and Mrs. A. J. Wilder a short distance East of

Mansfield. The rooms were prettily decorated with wild flowers of a yellow and green shade and red Autumn leaves. Roll call was responded to by giving some current event. The lesson for study and discussion was on Italy, which was very interesting.

During the social hour music on the victrola was enjoyed, and the hostess assisted by Mrs. N. J. Craig served a bountiful two course luncheon to the following members. . . .

All present declared it a most pleasant event and departed for their homes at a late hour.

Laura helps dedicate library here in 1951

SEPTEMBER 18, 1986
(Reprinted from the October 4, 1951 issue of the *Mansfield Mirror*.)

As Mrs. Wilder became a nationally recognized author, Mansfield was slow in seeing the ordinary woman they all knew as someone they too could recognize in a special way. In 1951 the Mansfield branch of the Wright County Library was rightly named, at its dedication, after their most famous citizen, with Mrs. Wilder present to be honored by her home town.

Mrs. Wilder loved the library and visited there often as Ms. Nava Austin tells us in chapter six. We can imagine what a special honor this library dedication was for her, maybe more so even than the library dedication she had attended two years earlier in Detroit. SH

Honoring a famous hometown writer of children's books, citizens of Mansfield Friday dedicated their branch of the Wright County library as the Laura Ingalls Wilder Library.

Librarians, school children, and longtime friends of Mrs. Wilder participated in the dedication ceremony which was held in the gymnasium of the Mansfield High School beginning at 2 p.m. Huge baskets of gorgeous autumn flowers decorated the stage and corridor of the building.

Grade school children marched into the auditorium and sang a greeting to Mrs. Wilder, who has become a nationwide favorite with boys and girls because of her books. The high school band played several selections. The Rev. Carlton Knight gave the invocation.

Mrs. Essa Findley, Wright County school superintendent, presided. She gave a brief history of Mrs. Wilder's career—how 57 years ago a home-hunting couple with a small daughter drove into Mansfield in a covered wagon. They were seeking relief in the Ozarks from many hard winters and three years of dry summers in South Dakota.

The young wife turned her eyes toward an inviting green wooded hill on which was situated a little school of the town. "Here," she said hopefully, "is where we stop."

Her husband agreed, and they camped nearby until they had found a suitable homesite of 40 acres, one mile east of town. Only five acres of their homesite had been cleared and the only building on it was a one-room windowless log cabin with a fireplace. Mr. and Mrs. Wilder cleared the land and built a new home as soon as possible. Mrs. Wilder still lives on this home place, known as Rocky Ridge Farm. Her husband, Almanzo Wilder, died in 1949 at the age of 92. Their daughter, Rose Wilder Lane, now of Danbury, Connecticut, is a famous novelist and short story writer.

WROTE FOR NEWSPAPERS

(At the reception) Mrs. Findley (Wright County superintendent of schools) said that Mrs. Wilder began writing for magazines and newspapers shortly after she came to Mansfield. She was active in women's clubs, including the Athenian Club of which she was a charter member. It was organized in 1916 in Hartville and had as its goal the organization of a county library.

"Now," said Mrs. Findley proudly, Wright County has library branches in Hartville, Mansfield, Norwood, and Mountain Grove and a bookmobile which visits rural districts."

Among the honors she listed for Mrs. Wilder are an honorary membership in the Eugene Field Society of Authors and Journalists; her selection as favorite living author by Chicago school children in 1949; the designation of a handsome new branch library in Detroit as "The Laura Ingalls Wilder Library," in 1949; and the dedication of the "Laura Ingalls Wilder Children's Reading Room" in the Pomona, Calif., public library in 1950. . . .

Paxton P. Price, Missouri state librarian of Jefferson City, made the speech of dedication. He also presented the Laura Ingalls Wilder Memorial bookshelf, as spokesman for the 1950 convention of the Missouri Library Association which voted recognition to Mrs. Wilder as an outstanding children's author.

The association has provided an inscribed metal plate for the case which will include autographed copies of Mrs. Wilder's eight books and also some delightful figures school children have created to depict characters in the stories.

Recounting Mrs. Wilder's achievements as a writer, the state librarian stressed her place as a good neighbor in the community. He said

Mrs. Wilder was famous in her home community for her fine needlework and delicious gingerbread as well as for her literary achievements.

PAYS TRIBUTE TO AUTHOR

"Of the thousands here and abroad who know Mrs. Wilder through her books and covet our opportunity today, we are the privileged few who can pay personal tribute to this famous woman," he said.

"The appreciation and enjoyment of Mrs. Wilder's books became so universal that the public librarians, almost as one, came to realize their debt to this great Missouri author for her part in making their services successful."

Mrs. Wilder, a charming little white-haired woman, wore a dark red velvet dress and an on the shoulder orchid, a gift from the Wright County Library. She appeared far younger than her 84 years as she graciously responded to the tributes paid her. . . .

Mrs. Wilder's Pen Stilled At Age of 90

FEBRUARY 14, 1957

The obituary that the Mansfield Mirror *printed at Mrs. Wilder's death in 1957 was requested by many other newspapers, which caused the newspaper to print a follow-up article to the obituary about these requests a week later.* SH

While the pencil of Mrs. Laura Ingalls Wilder, 90, has stopped with her death, the works of that pencil will live on forever.

Mrs. Wilder, Mansfield's own internationally known authoress, died Sunday night at her home two miles east of Mansfield.

Mrs. Wilder, a resident of this community for over 60 years, came in 1894 with her husband, Almanzo Wilder, in a covered wagon from De Smet, South Dakota, because of a three-year drought. They lived in town for awhile and then acquired a nearby acreage.

In the earliest years they worked hard raising chickens and cattle, as well as tending fruit.

It was not until 1932 that her first book was published. Then it was not written with the idea of publication, but to preserve family stories. Her first book, "Little House in the Big Woods," was the story of her girlhood and that of her sister, Mary, in a log cabin in the big woods of Wisconsin near Lake Pepin. She used actual characters and events in the story.

The next books followed in rapid succession. They continued the account of herself and her three sisters, Mary, Carrie, and Grace, and their parents as they moved from one frontier settlement to another.

As the principal characters grew older, the books were published for older girls. The books continued through Mrs. Wilder's teaching career when she was 16 and her marriage to Almanzo Wilder, when sleigh rides and buggy rides figured in the romance. They were written after she was 65 years of age and since have been translated in German, Japanese, and Chinese, printed in Braille for the blind, and pictured on film for bedfast patients. It was estimated in 1953 that over half a million children had read the "Little House" [stories].

At the dedication of the local library, Sept. 28, 1951, in Mrs. Wilder's honor, the speaker pointed out that she also was famous in her own community for her fine needlework, delicious gingerbread and in general known as a good neighbor.

She was born Feb. 7, 1867, in the state of Wisconsin. She is survived by a daughter, Rose Wilder Lane of Danbury, Connecticut, well-known novelist.

Final rites were conducted at 2 o'clock Wednesday afternoon at the Mansfield Methodist church by the Rev. Walter Brunner, pastor. Burial was in the Mansfield cemetery. Services were in charge of Kelley-Ferrell-Conner funeral home.

Pallbearers were S. R. Craig, Wayne Tarbutton, W. C. Coday, Marvin Jones, Karl Tripp, and G. C. Freeman.

Author's Renown Shown in Scores of Letters Received

FEBRUARY 21, 1957

"We feel like we almost have lost a member of our own family."

This and similar messages of devotion were included in numerous requests from outstate for copies of the Mansfield Mirror which contained an account of the death a week ago Sunday of Mrs. Laura Ingalls Wilder, nationally known authoress.

Approximately 200 extra copies were sold. About a half were sent

directly from the office and others were purchased over the counter to be mailed by the individuals.

The written requests were sent from Iowa, South Dakota, Kansas, Montana, Washington, Minnesota, and Michigan. Seven of the requests were from Michigan and four from Minnesota.

The requests were not confirmed [sic] to any particular age group, but were largely from teachers and parents. But all were "devout fans of Mrs. Wilder's from her first book published." All elaborated upon their devotion.

One school teacher took four pages of note paper to tell of not only her personal loss, but of the other five third grade teachers in her building that "mourned her passing." One of these teachers had written Mrs. Wilder seven years ago and received a "much treasured answer." She also added that she and her family were making plans to visit Missouri and the home of Mrs. Wilder.

A writer from Kansas mentioned that they had not only taken their children to De Smet, South Dakota, to see the landmarks mentioned in her books but had visited her personally in Mansfield three years ago.

"I am beset by questions regarding her and her family, as a teacher who loves to share her wonderful books with the children," wrote a Michigan teacher. A Minnesota teacher in addition to purchasing materials regarding this well-known writer wanted to purchase colored slides of her and her home in Mansfield.

Pictures taken on a trip to De Smet, South Dakota, former home of the Wilders, were included in one of the letters sent to the Mirror. One was of the bank building or the original store building where the family lived during the hard winter about which the internationally

known authoress wrote. Another was of a historical marker outside of the city informing tourists that this town was the setting of Laura Ingalls Wilder's stories and the birthplace of her daughter, Rose Wilder Lane.

In a long article in The De Smet News, which the Mirror received, it stated that "Mrs. Wilder was the daughter of Mr. and Mrs. Charles P. Ingalls, first family to reside in De Smet when it was established in 1880. Laura attended the first public school here, taught rural school, and married Almanzo J. Wilder, a pioneer settler. They left De Smet in 1896 [1894] by team and wagon with their baby daughter, Rose, for southern Missouri.

"It was years later that the mother became known as a writer. She had conducted a children's department for a southern farm magazine when she undertook to put down on paper the pioneering of the Wilder and Ingalls families in New York state, Wisconsin, Kansas, Minnesota, and Dakota Territory. They were published by Harper & Brothers in [a] series of eight books and have had several republications."

The four stories of De Smet are "By the Shores of Silver Lake," "Little Town on the Prairie," "The Long Winter," and "Those Happy Years" *["These Happy Golden Years"]*.

The article went on to say that Mrs. Wilder's books are the most popular in America.

When Mansfield decided to do a centennial album of the history of the town from 1882–1982, Mansfield: First One Hundred Years, *Laura Ingalls Wilder and Almanzo James Wilder figured prominently in it. In the next piece, Debbie Von Behren, award-winning high school teacher, native of the town, and free-lance writer, summarized the meaning of Mrs. Wilder's*

presence in and about the town for the many purchasers of the town history who knew its most famous citizen only by name.

LAURA INGALLS WILDER, OUR SPECIAL LADY

As I look out the back window of my home in the small town of Mansfield, Missouri, I can see the grave of one of the world's most famous and beloved authors.

However, even though Laura Ingalls Wilder has been dead for 25 years, it is not an exaggeration to say she still lives on. How many of us Mansfield kids can remember being given one of the "Little House" books for a birthday or Christmas, reading the dust cover, and being impressed that the lady who wrote the book had lived in the same town that we lived in. How many of us remember going on a field trip with our class from school and walking through the house she had lived in. At the time, that was pretty heady stuff, and we enjoyed having a famous person linked to our town.

Yet, back then, we didn't truly realize the importance of what Laura had done, what an impact she had on the world of literature. We also didn't know that in the '70s, Laura Ingalls Wilder would be a name known to virtually every child and adult in America.

Although Laura's medium was the printed word, the medium that made her name a household word was television. In 1973, Mansfield residents were delighted to find that Laura's books were going to be the basis for a television series. With already established actor Michael Landon heading the project, and a young girl named Melissa Gilbert portraying Laura, the show was an instant hit, and has turned into one of television's longest running, most successful series.

However, most people that know anything about Laura's life realize that most of what has been on "Little House on the Prairie" is total fiction. The series has not remained true to Laura's books. But even so, there have been good side effects. Everyone, and I don't think everyone is too much of an overstatement, now knows who Laura Ingalls Wilder was. Her books have become more popular than ever before. They are a staple on bookstore shelves, and virtually every school child in America has been exposed in some way or another to one of her books.

Laura's books were written for children, but you don't have to be a child to enjoy them. Practically every winter, down they come from my shelf. As I read them from cover to cover, I marvel at the simple storytelling skill Laura had, the ability to allow the reader to experience the sights, sounds, smells, and tastes of what she describes.

And now when I try to write myself, I think about how hard and frustrating it is to get the words to convey what I want them to say, and how easy Laura's writings make it seem. Hers was a rare talent, and combined with the special times she grew up in, a magic combination exists forever in the pages of her books.

Laura's books are pleasant literary diversions, but they also are teachers of the old-fashioned values of respect, truthfulness, honest labor, family pride, and love for our fellow man. At a time when many children don't get much moral training from their families, her books can show children that they should obey their parents, that they should always tell the truth, that they should help people who are in need.

We aren't the only town in America to claim Laura Ingalls Wilder for our own. Every community she has lived in wants some of the glory of having had a famous citizen. Well, I hate to disappoint them, but I think

Laura especially belongs to Mansfield. She and Almanzo chose our town, she lived here for over 60 years, and most important, she wrote every single one of her books here.

We know Laura was special. But there also has to be something special about the town that provided the environment necessary for her talent to shine through.